What Happened to Kitty

BLACKIE & SON LIMITED
50 Old Bailey, LONDON
17 Stanhope Street, GLASGOW

BLACKIE & SON (INDIA) LIMITED
Warwick House, Fort Street, BOMBAY

BLACKIE & SON (CANADA) LIMITED
TORONTO

C 781

"THE PLACE IS BURNED DOWN!"

What Happened to Kitty

BY

THEODORA WILSON WILSON

Author of "The Children of Trafalgar Square"
"Cousins in Camp" "Jim's Children" &c.

BLACKIE & SON LIMITED
LONDON AND GLASGOW

Blackie's
Imperial Library

The Treasure of Clint. G. I. Whitham.

Lydia Gaff. Violet M. Methley.

The Adventurous Seven. Bessie Marchant.

The Boys of Castle Cliff School. R. A. H. Goodyear.

Ann's Great Adventure. E. E. Cowper.

The Golden Magnet. G. Manville Fenn.

Every Inch a Briton. Meredith Fletcher.

'Twixt Earth and Sky. C. R. Kenyon.

In the Musgrave Ranges. Jim Bushman.

No Ordinary Girl. Bessie Marchant.

Norah to the Rescue. Bessie Marchant.

What Happened to Kitty. Theodora Wilson Wilson.

Printed in Great Britain by Blackie & Son, Ltd., Glasgow

Contents

Contents

WHAT HAPPENED TO KITTY

CHAPTER I

The Last of That!

"POOR Miss Kitty—she has a rare nerve!"

Mr. Roper, the riding-master, sighed heavily.

He was watching a slender bare-headed girl of fourteen, as she sat tightly and easily on a big horse, sending him backwards and forwards over the centre hurdle at the riding-school.

"And well she may!" he muttered. "Daughter of the neatest rider who ever sat a horse! Poor lady—Mrs. Threlby will never sit a saddle again!"

"There!" The girl pulled up in front of him, and, flinging her right leg backwards, she sprang lightly to the ground. "That is the last of that!" She patted the damp neck of the shrewd old horse, and forced a queer kind of a smile at the riding-master.

"Yes," he admitted reluctantly, "but there will be a stable full of horses where you are going, Miss, and we shall be hearing that Miss Threlby of Threlby End is the Queen of the Westmorland Hunt!"

Kitty made no answer, but flicked off some fragments of peat dust from her shabby gaiters.

"And when you are back in London, you won't forget the old man who has given you so many stiff drillings? You'll come and show him what a grand lady you are, eh?"

"Mr. Roper—don't," said Kitty. "I hate it all. I'd stay here for good if I could—I'll never, never find anyone so kind as you in Westmorland."

"Nonsense!" said the old man gruffly, as he took Kitty's outstretched hand. "Your poor mother did her duty as riding-mistress to the school, until she dropped, and if you had been older you might have taken her place and welcome. But you're too young, Miss, that's your worst fault, and it's best that you should go where you will be properly taken care of."

"I wonder," sighed Kitty. "I'm sure I look seventeen! I am sick already of being that horrible old squire's niece—so there! I shall return before you know where you are, and you will have to find me a job, or—or I'll run away with one of your horses and join a circus!"

"Right you are, Miss," he said vehemently. "And now you must take a run round the stables, to see the last of them all."

"It will have to be a run," said Kitty ruefully, and away they went.

A little later Kitty left the riding-school and hurried along until she came to a small second-hand book shop. She slipped past the group of idlers who were turning the books over at the door, and entered the dingy place.

"Ah!" said an old man, looking up from his desk with brightening eyes. "It's you, Miss Kitty?"

"Yes, it's me," said the girl. "I have had my last ride, and now I want my last go on the fiddle."

"Yes, yes," said Mr. Reuben Steiner. "Horse or fiddle? Fiddle or horse? Which is it? A horse may deceive you, but a fiddle never—never!"

He peered at her over his glasses, and rose rheumatically.

He was obviously a Jew, and he spoke with a foreign accent, and Kitty used to laugh with her mother, and say that her only chums in the wide world were two old men!

Reuben Steiner called gruffly to a weak-eyed youth to look after the door, to see that no books were stolen, and then he led his young visitor into his inner den.

This "den" was as crowded as the shop, with books mounted high in dangerously shaky piles, and queer old prints in shabby frames leaning against the walls.

But what did the stuffy scent of books or the dimness of the light matter to these two? Kitty knew exactly where to find the fiddle, and after taking it out of its case, and unfolding the silk handkerchief carefully, she rested it on her uplifted knee, tuned it, and then nestled it into her neck.

"I'll just play anything that comes into my head," she said. So she played on and on, interrupted now and then by a grumpy remark from Mr. Steiner, who sat for the most part with his forehead clasped between his hands.

An ancient clock gave forth a hiccoughing sound. It was four o'clock.

"That is the last of that!" said Kitty, as she laid the fiddle on the old man's knee.

"But it's not the last of that," he said, lifting the precious instrument and running a grimy finger along the shining wood. "No, little lady, you may be going off—who knows where?—but the old fiddle would cry in her case if she were left behind! Take her with you, little lady, you'll tend her as I have tended her, and some time you'll bring her back and let her sing to the old man once more, eh?"

Kitty's eyes filled with sudden tears.

"Oh, I wish I weren't going! Why can't I stay in London?"

But the old book-dealer shook his head.

"No, no! It is best as it is. We're all glad enough that you've found someone to take care of you."

"Mr. Steiner! That is just what Mr. Roper said. Why have you all gone mad on thinking I want someone to take care of me?   I feel fifty!"

Yet Kitty's comical smile came, even through the tears.

"Well, well, little lady," said the old man kindly. "We won't spoil the last minutes with a quarrel."

"And it is the last minute!" groaned Kitty, looking at the clock. "Any minute that housekeeper person may be coming to drag me away. Now, don't you think——"

"Yes, little lady?"

"That my uncle might have come himself? Don't you think he might have come to the funeral? Don't you think he might have come to see us when—when Mother was here?"

"When your own sweet mother was here, little lady," mused the old man, "I have heard her say many a time, when I've been on with my grumbles: 'Mr. Steiner, when things go crooked, hope for the best; and when people go wrong, hope for the best.'"

"I know—but then Mother was an angel!" said Kitty tremulously.

Mr. Steiner was folding up the fiddle in the purple handkerchief, and fitting it into the old case.

"Here she is, little lady! Who should have her more than you, eh? It was your mother who brought many a ray of light into this poor old heart of mine, and your mother's daughter—well, she is like my own!"

"Oh, Mr. Steiner, I don't know what to say!" declared Kitty, as she took up the treasure.

But they were interrupted by the entrance of Miss James—dear red-faced Miss James, the landlady who had been so truly kind to Kitty all through the trouble of her mother's illness and death.

"She's come!" she said in a sepulchral voice.

Kitty flushed anxiously. She knew that her uncle's housekeeper from Westmorland had come to drag her away.

CHAPTER II

Who is She?

THE doctor's boys, or "them two lads", as they were called in the village, made a rush for the local "slug" for Morley, and Roddy threw open the carriage door with a hinge-straining fling.

"Here you are, Mother!"

Mrs. Webster got in, closely followed by Nell M'Leod, the quarry owner's daughter. Then Roddy and Tim struggled for the right of way, and Tim won, as he generally did, and secured the far corner facing the engine.

The seat opposite to Tim was already occupied, and as Roddy planted himself close to Nell, he remarked under his breath:

"See my champion?"

Now Roddy, Tim, and Nell had had rather an exciting day.

Early that morning they had started out from Morley to "look after" Mrs. Webster, who had not only undertaken to be present at the gymnastic display and the exhibition of arts and crafts at the High Rigg Girls' School, but was also to distribute the prizes later in the afternoon.

Everyone called Mrs. Webster a delightful little

woman, but she was chiefly famed in the district because she happened to be the mother of Roddy and Tim.

A day off at High Rigg was always a joy, but at first the boys had been aggravatingly dubious as to whether they would care about watching a "pack of girls" display themselves.

"There is not the least need for you to give yourselves a Saturday's martyrdom!" their mother had remarked squashingly. "Nell will be quite capable of supporting me through my labours!"

"Rather!" Nell had answered eagerly, as she sat astride the window-sill of The Warren lounge. One bare leg was inside the room, and the other hung dangerously near the newly-bedded geraniums, as she pretended to be enjoying a fat green gooseberry.

"Decide—that is all I ask you!" added Mrs. Webster. She hated shilly-shallying, as was well known in the family.

Nell was Mr. Ian M'Leod's only child. Her mother had been dead for some years, and she and her father lived at the Pump House at the far end of the village, but it was extraordinary how much of her time she managed to put in at The Warren. She and Roddy were fourteen, Tim was thirteen, and the three squabbled away together quite as well as could be expected.

Nell had for some time posed as a despiser of girls and all their works, and had so far been educated at home, but she had been so thoroughly stirred by the boys' scorn of Miss Mason's School

at High Rigg, that she had rebelliously gone over
heart and soul to her sex, and was becoming as
delightfully rageous as the most up-to-date Suffragette.

On this day of days Nell had firmly made up
her mind that life alone with a governess was an
abomination and an insult to her fourteen years,
and that her father's life must be made a burden to
him until he allowed her to go to school.

Nell had suffered most healthfully at the Exhibition; for, secretly rather conceited over her various
accomplishments, she had felt all her spirit ooze
out of her as she saw the needlework, the plant
collections, the drawings, the wood-carving, and
watched the gymnastics, listened to the music, and
stared entranced at the acting. Nell had always
fancied herself in acting, but the way Roddy's
"champion" acted Volumnia in *Coriolanus* left
her limp.

It had, however, been some consolation to stroll
about with Mrs. Webster, the principal lady of the
day; and even now, as Nell lolled back in her
corner, she was greatly enjoying the exquisite
bouquet of roses which had been presented to
Mrs. Webster by the "youngest child in the
school".

As Roddy whispered his remark, Nell looked
across at the girl seated opposite to Tim.

During the gym. display the three had amused
themselves by selecting their champions, and
Roddy had waxed enthusiastic over a tall, slender
girl with rather a white face and sunken grey eyes,

and a lot of dark hair which frizzed itself in tiny waves about her forehead.

Roddy's choice had been fortunate, for his champion had won the high jump with an ease which flushed his cheeks with excitement. Higher and higher the rod was raised, and while the other girls, in spite of their furious and ungainly efforts with arms and shoulders, gradually fell back discomfited, this girl, without the least bustle or apparent anxiety, leaped two inches higher than any of her companions, amidst wild applause from girls and visitors.

Her efforts on the horse and the horizontal bar were equally bewildering, while during the concert she made Roddy feel positively queer down his backbone! Was her fiddle bewitched?

To her admirer's disappointment, she only received one small prize, for botany, yet the girls clapped her as though she had been head of the school—far more, indeed, than they clapped the fair, freckly girl whom Tim had selected, who won a whole armful of prizes.

By means of the programme the three discovered that the girl's name was Katherine Threlby, and, now that they were in the train together, they would like to have smiled an acquaintance.

But she sat quiet and impassive, with a sort of severely snubbing expression on her face, as though, indeed, she declined to admit that anyone was in the carriage.

"Now, children, subside!" said Mrs. Webster rather wearily as she opened a newspaper.

"Right, Mamma!" said Tim, with a wicked twinkle in his eye as he tugged from a misshapen pocket a horrible little rag, bearing the ominous name of *Lots o' High Jinks*.

"Tim!" exclaimed his mother. "I am ashamed of you!"

"Sorry I can't hide it inside a *Strand*, Mamma. But I'll spare it to you for five minutes—just to change the current of your thoughts!" And he slid along the seat and laid the paper on his mother's knee. "You must be awfully fed up with making pretty speeches and listening to them," he added in a whisper.

"Thanks!" and she glanced down the front page, filled with crude sketches of practical jokes. Then she shook her head.

"No—I can't! I really can't! Millions spent in education, and yet the schoolboy truly thinks this stuff funny!"

"Frizzled up into a worm on a gridiron, Tim!" remarked Nell triumphantly. "Do let me look, Madam Dear!" Nell used her pet name for Mrs. Webster.

But the train started with a jerk, and Nell's attention was attracted to Kitty, for she noticed that the girl pulled round a heavy bag from her shoulder, and brought out a pencil, a notebook, and some sort of arithmetic book.

She began busily writing down figures, and her lips moved involuntarily as she now and again stared out of the window, and, to Nell's joy, she began moving her fingers mysteriously, after a manner that this young person well understood.

"She's a human soul!" thought Nell, and from watching her fingers Nell took to examining her clothes.

She noticed that, like the rest of the girls, Roddy's champion was dressed in white; but she also saw that the muslin was of a very well-washed quality, and that there was a tell-tale mark near the hem where it had been let down, while the school hat, stuck so very far back on her head, had seen many a storm.

The white frock was partly covered by a faded black coat, and the only parts of her outfit to admire were the neat black stockings and shoes.

This girl had certainly very well-shaped legs, and Nell envied them with a sigh, for she herself was plumping out dreadfully, and was secretly taking lemon and hot water every night to make herself thin.

When Nell had examined all there was to be seen, and had puzzled greatly as to why any girl should bother about lessons on the evening of an entertainment, she turned to giggle with the boys over *High Jinks*.

Presently the girl closed her books sharply, stuffed them into her bag, and pulled the strap through with unnecessary vigour.

The train slowed down, and she rose to take her fiddle-case from the rack.

Roddy leaned out and opened the door for her. She gave him the stiffest nod in acknowledgment;

then suddenly her face lighted up with a sunny smile and she walked away.

"So she lives at Boardale!" exclaimed the boy, as he sat back again.

"Don't think much of your champion's manners," said Tim. "She's a stick! Just a stick!"

"More like a magic wand!" retorted Roddy aggressively, for he had seen the smile. "Did you ever see a stick jump as she did?"

"Her frock has been let down," remarked Nell.

"You think of nothing but clothes," said Roddy. "You're simply hipped on clothes!"

"Don't squabble," suggested Mrs. Webster. "We are all too tired. Oh——"

"What is it, Mamma?" cried Tim.

"It is supposed that Suffragettes have blown up another lovely old mansion."

"Where, Mother?" cried Roddy, leaning over to read the paper.

"In the Midlands. We women must have votes, but this is too futile."

"Women want boiling in liquid oil!" announced Tim sweepingly.

"Liquid oil!" sneered Nell. "If it wasn't liquid, how could it be oil?"

"Might be frozen," said Tim squashingly.

"Frozen and boiling!" broke in Roddy more squashingly.

"It is the women who have all the pluck nowadays," asserted Nell.

"Sick of 'em!" said Tim grandly. "Females

on the war-path never could play the game.
Always want to be at the wicket and stick their
skirts in front, and then shout out that it wasn't
l.b.w.!"

"I'll never, never bowl for you again!" said
Nell, flinging off her hat and shaking her head
at him.

"Yes; and if we took to hullabalooing over
everything we wanted and couldn't get——" began
Roddy.

"We'd get jolly well licked," said Tim.   "And
if we did get a licking, you wouldn't hear us yelling
all over the place like a silly female."

This was probably true from the boy's point of
view, for Tim was personally plucky in pain, and
had borne his full share of school thrashings with
stolid nerve.

"Well—anyhow," said Nell, "men have been
grabbing and grabbing for millions and millions
of years, and it's quite time that someone showed
them that they can't have every single thing their
own way.   I'll start a League amongst the rising
generation," Nell added keenly; "and I believe
that girl would join—she's just the sort."

"We're sick of the whole subject," said Roddy
cuttingly.   "Is there anything in the paper about
the scheme, Mother?"

"A little," and she pointed to a paragraph.

"Oh, let's see!" exclaimed the others.

The Websters and Nell entered very keenly into
the life of their district, and the latest rage was in
connection with a proposed Model Village, which

Mr. M'Leod was planning to build for the quarry-men.

Dr. and Mrs. Webster had groaned for long over the state of the cottages in Morley, and they and Mr. M'Leod and several others had designs for forming a company called " Morley Model Village, Limited ".

Sheets and sheets of paper had been sacrificed at the Pump House and at The Warren in drawing designs to make the most of the site at the least possible cost.

Nell was all for cupboards, and having triumph-antly arranged for four good ones in each cottage, she had been covered with confusion at finding she had forgotten to leave a space for the stairs.

In spite of the discovery that it wasn't quite so easy as it looked to plan a perfect cottage, all had gone swimmingly on paper; but this week a great blow had fallen upon the schemers. The particular piece of land they wanted was called the Fold Field, and belonged to Mr. Jonathan Threlby of Threlby End.

Mr. Threlby lived a retired life, about four miles away from Morley, and, to Mr. M'Leod's genuine surprise, he had, through his lawyer, absolutely declined to sell the property or to take any part in the improvement scheme.

The fury of the children at this unexpected baulk can be imagined, and at the least encouragement they would have been prepared to gallop off to Threlby End and present pistols at Mr. Threlby's head.

Dr. Webster, however, remarked that that was not the way they did things nowadays, and reminded them that Mr. Threlby's land happened to be his own.

"Just read it out, Mamma," said Tim.

"We understand that Mr. M'Leod and Dr. Webster are interested in a new scheme for removing the scandal of Morley Cottage property from our midst. We regret to learn, however, that this laudable project is being frustrated by a certain local landlord."

"He's just a cowardly brute!" said Tim irately. "Why doesn't he come out into the open and show himself? He daren't face your father, Nell, and so he sneaks behind a lawyer."

"He wants a couple of ferrets to unearth him," laughed Roddy.

"But if Father can't get the land, it will be U P," groaned Nell.

"It's just monstrous!" said Roddy. "We simply must have the land, with room for decent gardens for everyone."

"It isn't always such a simple thing to put wrong right in this world," warned Mrs. Webster quietly.

"No; I suppose we can't just slap-dash along anyhow," said Tim, with a sigh.

"Still, we must have the people happily housed," said his mother resolutely. "We cannot have every tourist who comes into our district pointing the finger of scorn. Besides, we point the finger of scorn at ourselves."

"We'll do the old wretch somehow," said Tim joyously.

"But, Mother!" exclaimed Roddy. "Katherine Threlby! Do you think that my champion can belong to him?"

"I really don't know, dear. It is possible; but Mr. Threlby lives such a strange retired kind of a life that I have not happened to hear of any young girl living with him."

"We must find out," said Roddy. And he meant what he said.

CHAPTER III

Three Miles to Threlby End

KITTY had now been at Threlby End for about a year, and had never failed, whether in rain or shine, snow or mist, to walk her three miles to Boardale station and back during term time.

Close to the station there was a public-house and a few cottages, but as Kitty turned south she faced the wild open country, over which at times the gales swept triumphantly. Her way lay at first along a well-kept road, with wide hillocky grass margins on which bramble and wild raspberry bushes flourished, and which were, on this early June evening, all gay with gorse and broom and ragged robins and wild geraniums, and many another summer flower.

The road was solitary, save for an occasional motorist who swept the dust into Kitty's eyes; but she strode along with a light easy pace, choosing the grassy margins, and only stopped for a moment as she passed a tumble-down cottage in which old Belle Catteral passed a strange witch-like existence.

Belle was standing at her gate, scraping a few

new potatoes and throwing them into a battered dish, as Kitty went by.

"Thoo's late to-night, lass!" she called. "Is ta over late to play me a tune?" and she eyed Kitty's fiddle-case.

"I am afraid I am," said Kitty pleasantly. "You are lucky to get new potatoes."

"Graved t' ground myself, and graved them up myself, and it's myself that is going to eat 'em," she answered. "But never a taste o' butter. And what is new potatoes without a taste o' fresh butter?" So the old body ended up querulously.

"I'll see if I can bring you a taste on Monday," said Kitty. "Good-night!" and she hurried off.

After a long mile, Kitty turned due west, up a narrower road which mounted slowly upwards towards some distant fells.

She jerked her bag more comfortably on her shoulder, and changed the fiddle-case to the other hand.

Her face was grave as she tramped along, yet now and again she raised her eyes to the sweet June sky, now subtly changing from an everlasting blue to a vague ruddy grey.

"Preparing the way for the sunset," thought the girl. She smiled a little, and the frown on her broad brow uncreased.

It was towards the end of the second mile that Kitty, in spite of her burdens, began to quicken her pace, and at a certain turn in the road she sent forth a low musical whistle.

It had, perhaps, scarcely needed the whistle to

rouse a rough-coated Irish terrier to instant attention, as he lay on a bank some distance in front.

His brown body trembled in palpitating excitement, yet he remained where he was, as though held in some iron grip.

Even when he saw his mistress quite clearly, he did not advance, though he uttered three short irrepressible yelps.

"All right, Don!" laughed the girl, and Don shot towards her like a stone from a catapult.

Each morning Don followed Kitty to this trysting-place, and then, at her command, he would turn homewards with three inches of tail cuddled against him.

Every afternoon he trotted out again, as careless of the weather as his mistress, yet he never dared to come beyond this particular spot.

"Oh, Don, darling!" Kitty flung herself down on a slab of slate, under a flaming bush of broom, which scattered a shower of petals over her shoulder by way of gay greeting.

"Did it seem very long to you, to-day—you poor darling?"

Kitty was two hours later than her usual time, yet she had known that Don would keep a true vigil.

Don now merely wagged what man had left him of his tail, and went on with his occupation of licking his mistress's hands and arms as high up as he could reach. All the anxiety of his doggish heart was forgotten, now that he was pawing her coat and her frock.

"Everything just as usual, I suppose, old man?"
she remarked, as at last she rose. It seemed a
pity that Don could not speak. He could tell her
nothing.

Kitty now hurried on, for she wanted her supper
badly. Her tea at school had only been a bite and
a promise, for the girls had been expected to wait
on the visitors, rather than to look after themselves.

The road descended sharply, cutting through an
oak and a hazel plantation—a tangle of young
green, with entrancing peeps of blue hyacinths and
primroses—a fairy wood in all truth.

A rabbit scuttled across the road. Don leaped
forward and disappeared in full cry, to return in a
few moments with his quarry.

"Oh, Don! You'll be hanged for murder some
day," said Kitty, as she stooped and took the warm
limp body of the young rabbit from him.

Don looked a little crestfallen, and walked slowly
by his mistress's side, only venturing now and
again to take a refreshing sniff at the treasure.

Presently a gate barred the way. Kitty opened
it and Don squashed himself under it. They had
now left the wood for an open road, bounded on
one side by some low-lying ground, a stream, and
a wide fell which stretched to the sunset, while to
their right there was a thick yew fence, about six
feet in height, extending for about two hundred
yards.

Kitty reached a wide gate, greatly in need of a
coat of paint, and, opening it, she turned up the
weedy drive.

Magnificent evergreens rose from the deep hay-grass, while rhododendrons in full flower massed themselves gloriously to her right.

The drive curved upwards to a rambling two-storied house of very ancient appearance, but Kitty passed the wide oak door, so thickly studded with nails, and went round into a grass-grown stable-yard, where she made for a colour-washed porch, against which there lay some brightly burnished pans.

She stopped short in the yard and listened, without exactly knowing why.

It suddenly felt to her as though a strange unearthly silence brooded over the place, and Don watched her anxiously.

At her first footfall in the yard, Marjory, the tall capable housekeeper who ran the whole domain, was accustomed to hurry out to greet Miss Kitty with respectful and friendly assurance that supper was waiting, while in stormy weather dry clothing was always ready for her.

But Marjory was not there, so Kitty went through the porch and entered the kitchen.

Supper was laid on a cloth of finest linen, the peat fire was glowing, and some bread was down by the hearth, waiting to be made into toast.

Kitty walked across the flagged floor to the hearth-rug. Then she looked towards the door that led to the house.

"Don!" and she gave a little forced laugh. "Am I bewitched to-night, or is there something the matter?"

Then the door opened slowly, and Marjory entered.

"Ah! it is you, Miss Kitty!" she said in an unusually low tone.

"Why, who else could it be?" asked Kitty, now really startled.

"No, no, who else could it be? That is just what I told the master. He—well, he's a bit worried this evening, Miss Kitty."

"That is nothing new," said Kitty, rather hardly. "And here's a rabbit to keep us out of the workhouse!"

"You look tired, Miss Kitty," said Marjory, changing the subject abruptly. "I'll have your supper ready in a few minutes."

"I had better go and say 'Good evening' to Uncle Jonathan first," said Kitty.

"No—not now—I wouldn't," said Marjory, a trifle anxiously. "Have your supper in peace. You are late, and—and I want to get my kitchen cleared."

"There is something wrong, Marjory!" exclaimed Kitty, laying her hand on the woman's arm. "Do you think I am a bat? Tell me!"

"No—no indeed, Miss Kitty, there is nothing wrong!" said Marjory earnestly. "Only—well—you know it is late, and the master likes his evening pipe in peace."

"The bat sees!" said she, in a little tone of mockery, not in the least believing Marjory's excuse. Then flinging her hat, coat, and bag on the window-seat, she sat down in the old rocking-chair, thankful to rest.

Marjory generally took her knitting, and occupied a stiff Windsor chair near the door, while Kitty ate her supper.

It was a joy to her in her solitary life to listen to the news that Kitty brought in from the outside world. But to-day, as soon as she had brewed the tea and boiled the eggs, she left her young mistress alone.

Kitty poured out her tea rather absently, and then opened her *Euclid*.

"In a month, Don, if I have luck, I shall be clear of all this," she said, as she gently stroked the soft head of the dog, who had seated himself hard against her legs.

Something in her tone made Don look up wistfully.

"It's not the remotest good to grump at me, old man!" she mocked him. "Heavy pathetic, and all that kind of thing! Of course if I win the scholarship I shall have to leave you for ages at a time; but if you could understand, you old silly, you would forgive me. You were never shunted into a house where nobody wants you! You were never forced to take what somebody hates to give you! You haven't to say 'thank you' to somebody for what you loathe to take! You even earn your own scraps! You can catch rabbits and rats, and keep tramps away. But I do nothing but cost!"

Then suddenly Kitty was aware that the door had opened softly, and that a man stood in the kitchen.

Whether he had heard what she said, she could not tell, but she rose with flushed cheeks.

The man was tall and striking-looking, with deeply-set eyes, a Roman nose, and a well-shaped and clean-shaven mouth and chin.

His shoulders were bent, however, and his dark hair was tinged with grey, though he was not much more than fifty years old.

He was wearing a shabby dinner jacket, black trousers, a spotless white shirt, and much-worn patent-leather shoes.

"Good evening, Katherine," he said ceremoniously. Then he added, in a complaining tone, which always set Kitty on edge, "You are very late."

"Yes, Uncle Jonathan, I explained to you that I should be late to-day. We had our mid-term Exhibition."

She was now standing with one arm raised to the high mantelshelf, and in the darkening room her face was not clear.

"I don't approve of young girls walking on the public road so late in the evening."

"If one cannot ride, one walks—naturally;" and Kitty gave rather a nervous little laugh. Yet she hated feeling nervous before Uncle Jonathan.

Her uncle looked at her with a curious intentness, as though he would like to read her through and through.

"Perhaps you would like me to provide you with a motor-car?"

"Oh, rather not, please, Uncle Jonathan!" she

exclaimed. "I loathe cars, and"—then coming impulsively forward she laid her hand on her uncle's arm—"Uncle Jonathan, some day I will pay back everything I have cost you. Some day I will earn money. If I win the scholarship I shall go away to school, and you will only be plagued with me in the holidays. Think of the joy of it!"

But there was no joy in her uncle's face at this unexpected outburst, and Kitty was too excited to notice how his lips worked with a scarcely suppressed agitation, and as he did not immediately reply, she went on recklessly:

"Good night, Uncle Jonathan. Please do not bother about me. I have piles of work to do to make up for this lost day."

But her uncle laid a heavy hand upon her thinly-covered shoulder.

"Katherine, I tell you I won't have it! It is absurd! Why should you worry over a miserable scholarship?"

Kitty gazed at her uncle in undisguised surprise.

"Why—so that—to save money, Uncle Jonathan! So that you may get rid of me!"

Her uncle dropped his hand, and turning away abruptly, he left her.

CHAPTER IV

Kitty Cannot Work

KITTY hurried off to her own room after supper, and, with Don as her companion, she collected a pile of books around her and sat down to work.

But to-night, though she scolded herself and stared at her books or scribbled down figures, she knew she was doing no good. Her brain was thinking of fifty other things—the prize-giving—the sports—those people in the train—her future life—her past life—anything and everything except Euclid's puzzles.

What years it seemed since she had ridden through the crowded London streets to that awful crowded cemetery, and had parted from her best friends, the riding-master, the horses, and the quaint old fiddler!

Marjory had been sent to London to fetch her, and at first Kitty scarcely cared what happened to her.

Yet the change from the bright scurrying life in London to the lonely house behind the yew hedge had been tremendous; but Kitty was full of pluck, and was, moreover, far too proud not to fall in with what was expected of her.

Marjory was always very kind, and Don was the greatest help in soothing the dreariness of her heart.

But Kitty had so thoroughly understood from her mother that Uncle Jonathan was rich beyond dreams, that it was a great shock to her to find that he was, or seemed to be, quite poor.

Though he possessed a house full of handsome furniture and beautiful pictures, he spent his life in a few rooms at the back. Though he had gardens and greenhouses he had no gardeners, but only one odd man named Samuel; and, worst of all, though he had stables, he had no horses.

This last had indeed been the real blow which Kitty could not get over, and she sometimes wandered through the empty stables longing—longing in vain—for the sound of the stamping hoof of a horse impatient for exercise, or for the feel of a soft nose through the loose-box bars.

No visitors ever came to the house, and only an occasional tradesman or farmer broke the silence.

Kitty had honestly tried to be "nice" to her uncle, but he had damped her friendliness from the very beginning. He treated her with a curious severe civility, and though he paid her school bills and her season ticket, he never allowed her to handle money. Now and then Marjory spoke to her master about Kitty's clothes, and he always told her to get what was necessary, but Kitty snubbed Marjory, and felt as though she would endure any shabbiness and any odd glances from the girls, rather than hint to her uncle that she needed anything.

So she mended her clothes, and let down her frocks, and scrubbed her hats and retrimmed them daintily, and longed like other girls for many things.

It was no small trial to mix with her school companions and never feel free to do as they did, but Kitty was such a general favourite that nobody seemed to mind.

She had set up a queer kind of friendship with old Belle Catteral, and the gossiping woman had told her strange tales of her uncle's wealth, and of how, ever since his wife's death, he had turned mean and miserly.

"Why, my dear, he grudges a drop of milk to the very cat on his hearthstone!" Belle had said one day.

"Nonsense!" Kitty had answered her; yet though she did not believe all that Belle said, her stories certainly helped to poison her mind against her uncle.

Kitty's greatest joy was in her fiddle; but even the fiddle had its drawbacks, for she had an uncomfortable impression that her uncle hated music; and, though it was necessary to practise, she had long ago learned to hide herself far away amidst the chintz-covered furniture in the drawing-room—all painted in gold and white.

Here she would draw aside the closed blinds, or, when dark, she would light a single candle on the music-stand.

Kitty had a queer sort of affection for this music-stand, and she used to wonder who had stood in front of it long ago, and who had filled this gaily lighted room with music for some brilliant company.

Now and then she would leave her fiddle, and, taking the candle, let the light fall on the face of a very beautiful woman whose portrait hung in a broad gilt frame in the centre wall between two mirrors.

Kitty guessed that this young girl in the riding-habit was her uncle's dead wife—her Aunt Molly.

If only that merry-eyed aunt had lived, what a difference she would have made in the old place!

But as a rule, when Kitty tucked her fiddle under her chin she forgot everything except the sheer joy in her art. She could not help knowing that she played well, and it was a consolation to feel that there was one subject in which she was not positively disgraced.

But Kitty little knew that, while thinking herself quite alone, her uncle often followed her, and sat in the darkness of the hall, listening with his head bent low in his hands.

Yet the moment Kitty stopped playing, he slipped away as though he were a dog caught stealing.

"Uncle Jonathan hates me and every mortal thing I do," Kitty sighed to herself, as she flung down her pencil. "I wonder why he plagued himself by asking me here! And why does he always look at me as if I were wrong somehow?"

Kitty started up, plunged a towel into her jug, wrung it out, and tied it round her head. Yet at the end of half an hour she had not won through a single problem.

" I wasn't built for mathematics, and that's the awful fact," she groaned, as she pitched the towel on to the floor. " Yet no one can pass exams unless they have some vague notion what happens when one adds two and two together! Two and two together! If I could do that, I might guess what is wrong in this queer house! Don!"

The dog started up and leaped tumultuously into her lap.

" Don!" and she kissed him affectionately; "what if I fail!" Her heart beat quicker, and she flushed up at the dreadful thought.

" It's just Uncle Jonathan who has got on my nerves," she argued. " I can't get the wretched man out of my head. I wish I knew whether Belle is right. Is he just a horrible miser?"

" Judge not, and ye shall not be judged. Give, and it shall be given unto you; good measure, pressed down, shaken together, and running over shall men give into your bosom." So the words came back to her, for they were favourite words of her warm-hearted mother.

" Kitty!" she would say. " It is always safest to think the best. If you want people to think the best of you, you must think the best of them. It is hard work—but it will make you the happiest in the end."

And so her mother had died, thinking the best of the husband who had promised her wealth and left her in poverty, and of her husband's brother, who had never once reached out a helping hand towards her in her need.

"It's no use," groaned Kitty. "I do want to think the best of Uncle Jonathan, but I can't. He is just keeping me like a charity girl!"

Then she got up and stretched herself wearily and did a few extension exercises.

"I know. I'll get a breath of fresh air in the garden," she exclaimed. "That will buck me up."

CHAPTER V

The Rose Garden

No sooner thought than done. A long June evening in the north is always entrancing, and though Kitty heard the grandfather's clock in the passage strike ten, it was not really dark.

There was plenty of tender colour left in the sky, as if the old day refused to extinguish its light until the new day had said good morning, and one sweet little evening star shone out, just as though he wanted to offer anxious-eyed Kitty a welcome.

Marjory had probably gone to bed, and her uncle would be grumping as usual in his study, so Kitty crept downstairs, and, going out at a side door, she wandered round towards the rose garden.

The rose garden in this neglected place had a strange fascination for Kitty. The beds had been laid out long ago in a symmetrical pattern, with flagged paths leading to the centre, in which there was a sun-dial surrounded by four stone seats.

Low walls partly surrounded it, over which the roses had scrambled, and you reached it by following a weedy path round by the front of the house, crossing a terrace and going down some broad steps.

Don was delighted to join in this unexpected excitement, and pranced about his mistress as though it had been daytime.

But Kitty had lost all fear of being out alone, for no one ever troubled to come to Threlby End; so she passed out to the terrace, and stood there a few moments, breathing in the refreshing air, and looking out towards the west, where Boar Fell cut the skyline.

It was all calm and peaceful and soundless, and the air was exquisitely scented with the multitude of flowers which managed to bloom amidst the neglect, perhaps in remembrance of the old glorious days of the past.

An owl's cry was rather startling. It was repeated several times and then it ceased altogether.

Kitty went down the steps so that she might smell the roses, and as she did so the dew-laden branches brushed against her muslin sleeves and cooled her arms.

She had reached the path, and was just going to walk across to the sun-dial, when she stopped short, and her heart began to beat most ridiculously.

There was someone sitting on the far seat, with his back towards her.

Don gave a sharp bark. The man turned.

"Oh, Uncle Jonathan!" gasped Kitty. "Is it only you?"

"Yes, it is only Uncle Jonathan," he said in a strange unusual kind of a voice, for he was quite as startled as his niece. "Come and sit down, my dear."

Amazed at his manner, Kitty came slowly forward, and sat down as far away from him as she could with any decency.

Perhaps her uncle noticed this, perhaps he didn't After a short pause, he said:

"Why are you here at this hour, my dear Katherine?"

"Oh, well, my brain was addled, and I couldn't work, and I adore this garden!" A sudden nonsensical fit came creeping over Kitty—a reaction from her grumps.

"I love this garden too," he said gravely.

Kitty couldn't imagine that Uncle Jonathan could love anything; but she didn't quite like to say so.

"I suppose," she began slowly, "this is where the Threlbys made love to each other and got engaged, and all that sort of thing?"

"Yes," he answered shortly.

Was it the influence of the sweet summer evening or the scent of the roses that was softening Kitty's heart to pity for her melancholy uncle? Perhaps her mother was right. Perhaps she oughtn't to judge. After all—even though Uncle Jonathan had not done as much for her as he might —still, he had done something. She might have been playing on the streets of London for a living, or riding as a circus girl, if he had not offered her the shelter of his strange home. And yet, what a pity he wasn't different—jolly like other peoples' uncles!

"Katherine, are you very miserable here?" he asked suddenly.

Kitty gasped, and, not having a moment to collect her wits, she blurted out: "Oh, no! This is a ripping place!"

The answer was not what he expected, and he turned a little as though he wanted to see her better.

"Still, you think I am hard on you?"

"Oh, well!" she stumbled rather badly. "Of course I can't expect you to be like my own splendid father."

"You were fond of your father?"

"He was a hero," said Kitty. "If he had only lived, I need not have troubled you."

"You do not trouble me, Katherine. That is your mistake. And I am sorry that you think me hard and mean. There have been reasons—I have not felt it right to be different."

Kitty could not imagine what her uncle meant by that, so she did not reply at all, but stroked Don rather violently down his backbone.

"You loved your mother dearly?"

"I would rather not speak about my mother, Uncle Jonathan," said Kitty sharply. "You despised her because she was once a circus girl. But she was the noblest and bravest woman who ever crossed a horse's back."

How she would like to have rushed out the old grievances! Had not her mother died because she had toiled at work for which she was not fit? Could not her uncle have found out how his own sister-in-law was getting on and helped her before it was too late? It was all abominable, and Kitty's soft feelings began to harden.

"I should like to have seen your mother ride," he said.

Kitty did not feel that this remark needed any answer. What had come over her uncle?

"When is your examination?" was his next astounding remark.

"Next week, Uncle Jonathan."

"If you wish to pass, I hope that you will pass, Katherine, but if by any chance you fail, don't worry."

Kitty felt her cheeks growing hotter and hotter. That was the most thoughtful thing her uncle had ever said to her.

Why could she not obey her mother and meet his friendliness by being nice to him?

"Of course I must worry," she said quickly. "I must worry until I am independent. I must have lots of money some day, and I am going to earn it all myself."

"You think that life is worthless without lots of money?"

"Everyone knows that," said Kitty certainly. "Not the money so much as the things that money will buy. I want beautiful things—beautiful clothes and beautiful everything! That is my ambition."

"Oh, Katherine!" He shrank back just as though she had struck him in the face.

His tone frightened her. She did not understand it, and she gave a nervous laugh.

"Anyway, I want beautiful horses," she insisted, "and if I don't get through my exam I will go off to be a riding-mistress. You asked me if I was happy

here, Uncle Jonathan—well, I'm not. I can't endure never, never to feel a horse under me. Good
night!"

"Katherine!" he exclaimed.

But Kitty had turned and run away, and the
man was left alone.

"I have played the coward again," he thought.
"Why dare I not tell her? How she hates and
mistrusts me!"

"And she is eating her heart out for the sake
of the horses," he muttered presently.

The wind stirred chillily. He went indoors and
re-read a letter which he had received that day from
a strange lawyer in London.

CHAPTER VI

An Evil Gossip

ON Monday Kitty remembered her promise to take some butter to old Belle.

But when she asked Marjory for it, the servant shook her head warningly.

"You are welcome to the butter, Miss Kitty," she said, "but you be advised by me, and steer clear of old Belle. She is a chattering mischief-maker, and as for cadging, she would beg from the man in the moon if she could get hold of him!"

Kitty laughed out.

"You needn't turn stingy," she retorted. "Belle is stuck away in that awful old hovel, and you needn't grudge her a few ounces of butter."

"Take the butter and welcome, if you promised it," answered Marjory; "but I'd advise you to take some cotton-wool with you, so that you can stop your ears when she begins her tales. Her tongue is poisoned—and that's the truth!"

So Kitty left the butter on her way to the station, and at night, disobeying Marjory's warnings, she called to hear from Belle how it had tasted.

"Oh, Miss Kitty!" cried the old woman. "It is you that I have been wanting to see all this blessed day!" and Belle forced some tears to her eyes and let them fall pathetically down her withered cheeks. "It's you that have come as an angel of light into the old house, to make up for the poor dead mistress. There was never such a lady as Mrs. Threlby. Bonny as the morning, and always ready to give a helping hand to the poor."

"Was my Aunt Molly very beautiful?" asked Kitty.

"Aye, lass! But"—and she dropped her voice—"not so bonny as you will be, lass, when you grow up and your fortune comes. You will be queen of all the countryside, let the Squire try to keep you down as he may, in them rags."

Kitty gave a laugh as she looked down at her shabby skirt, yet she flushed, too, for she knew she had no business to let Belle talk like that.

"Never mind me," she said hastily. "Tell me about Aunt Molly."

"Aye—why, she would drive along in her four-in-hand, holding the ribbons just as easy as a man. And she never minded how the money flew. There was always plenty to spare at Threlby when she was alive. She kept the Squire's pockets open. Parties and company and dancing. Why, I have danced there myself—me in my old cotton frock—and the mistress laughing fit to kill herself! But it's all over now. There is no dancing at Threlby now. Not unless it's the ghosts that dance, when they light up all them candles in the hall when you and the master are asleep. Can't you stop, Miss Kitty, and play me one tune for the sake of old times?"

Kitty laughed again, and, to humour the old woman, she took out her fiddle and played her a gay Irish reel, to which Belle beat time ecstatically with her hard, wizened hands.

"Ah, Miss Kitty!" she cried as the music stopped. "And your father was as beautiful as the mistress! I shall never forget the day when he found me gathering sticks on the fell, and gave me five shillings and a bonny smile to brighten them."

Kitty's eyes looked eager at the mention of her father, and Belle went on:

"Aye, it was sad work when the war took off the fine, handsome gentleman. It must be dree work living with such a man as the Squire—you being your father's own daughter. Folk says that the Squire begrudges the very firing from his own woods, and spreads the butter on your bread with his own hands."

"Belle, you are funny!" chuckled Kitty. "It isn't quite as bad as that." Still she was feeling uncomfortable, and was beginning to think that perhaps Marjory was right. "I really must go now," she said, as she shut up her case and swung her bag over her shoulder.

"Aye, you must go now, my bonny lass. Bless the light of your eyes and the shine of your hair; and good luck to the lass who can spare a smile for a poor old body like Belle."

"She is a queer old sort," thought Kitty, as she hurried off, anxious to make up for her wasted time.

CHAPTER VII

A Ride for Adventure

Now it was on the following Saturday that a great chatterment was going on in the village smithy.

Nell's horse, Nimrod, had cast a shoe, and she was waiting for him to be shod, while Roddy and Tim, having tied up their horses to a gate, were enjoying themselves in the smithy. Roddy was blowing the bellows, making a much bigger fire than the smith, Gregory, wanted; and Tim was searching about amongst a pile of fascinating scraps for something he needed to add to his elaborate railway system.

The three children, by dint of plaguing their respective parents to distraction, each possessed a horse, as all the countryside knew.

Nimrod, Rufus, and Hop-o'-my-Thumb could trot hard, face motors, let motor-cycles dash past them, cross country, and mount fells.

The boys rode three miles eastward to the Grammar School at Howard, and Nell cantered about a good deal alone; and the boys and she constantly sparred together as to whether she was, or was not, too hard on Nimrod.

"Women are always too hard on their horses," Roddy would remark, by way of throwing down the gauntlet.

"He loves cantering," Nell would snap back.

"But it is jolly hard for his legs on the roads, and you only make him do it because you are too lazy to trot," Roddy would answer back.

The three horses were light in build, and were kept in quite a simple way. The children usually saddled and bridled them themselves, and did a fair share of the grooming; but it must be confessed that the M'Leod's chauffeur, Thomas, and the doctor's odd man, Hughie, put a good many finishing touches.

"Hurry up, Mr. Gregory, do!" said Nell impatiently. "Time flies!"

"Aye, Time has always been ahead of flying-machines, let 'em bust theirselves as they may," said the smith imperturbably, as he hitched up Nimrod's off fore-hoof and supported it between his knees; "and Time has never broke down yet —not to my knowledge." He did not speed up in the slightest degree.

"But we want to keep up with him to-day," urged Nell. "We have such piles to do." She put her arm about the fidgety beast's neck, and drew her fingers through his mane.

"And where might you be going this time?" asked Gregory, as he shaved away at the horse's hoof with his sharp knife.

"Not a notion," said the girl. "That is the best of adventures. You never know. When we

A Ride for Adventure

come to cross-roads we shall let the horses choose
—turn and turn about."

"Hum! Then you won't get very far," grunted
the smith.

"Why?" asked Nell.

"You should be rider enough to know by this
time that horses will surely turn back to their own
stables as soon as the tickle has gone out of their
feet."

"Roddy and I are going by the way the wind
blows," said Tim, breaking in. "You know the
old saying:

'A boy's will is the wind's will,
   And the thoughts of youth are long, long thoughts.'"

"Never heard it afore," said Gregory frankly;
"but it's true enough. There is no getting to the
bottom of what a lad will be after. But think on't,
there's another good old saying:

'For want of a nail the shoe was lost,
   For want of a shoe the horse was lost,
   For want of a horse the rider was lost,
   For want of a rider the kingdom was lost,
   And all for want of a horse-shoe nail!'

Now, Miss Nell, do you still want me to hurry?"

"I really don't believe, when I come to watch
you, that you could hurry, Mr. Gregory," and
Nell's blue eyes sparkled with impudence. "So
sorry I worried you."

But the smith understood his youthful customer
by this time, and, letting the hoof drop so that he
might take up the shoe, he said coolly:

"Well, it's only by every man attending properly to his own job that the world is kept spinning. You can't get over that."

"And the women?" struck in Roddy.

"And the women," admitted the smith; "or where would my breakfast be?"

"That is the worst of men," said Nell, shaking her head scornfully, "always thinking about their —their insides."

"Oh!" mocked the boys. "That's good!"

"Very good!" said Tim solemnly. "Chocolates — ice - cream — cream buns — strawberries — sour gooseberries——"

"And the merrythought!" said Roddy.

"And shirking porridge!" said Tim.

"I wish you three would let me finish my sentence," remarked the smith. "It's a job to get in a word edgewise amongst this party. All I want to say is, that it's my job to see that you start out right. Then I won't be rolling on my bed and tearing my hair because any of you have come to grief."

The thought of the massive Gregory rolling on his bed and tearing his bald pate sent them off into disrespectful squeals of laughter, as the smith at last began to hammer in the nails with smart, accurate blows.

"And how is Morley Model Village, Limited?" he asked presently.

The children had often received warnings not to gossip indiscriminately as to what they heard at home, but Gregory was an exception to every rule; so Roddy felt at liberty to reply:

"You saw what the paper said last week?"

"Aye. We're getting a bit public in Morley, seemingly. But it doesn't take much to set a newspaper man's pen going nowadays. It's the invention of these here fountain-pens that likely does it—can't stop 'em running."

"Well, what the paper said that time was true," said Roddy. "We're stuck. We can't get land at any price."

"But we aren't going to be stuck," said Nell. "My father will leave no stone unturned."

"Aye. Well, your father has moved a deal of stones in his time," Gregory admitted; "but I doubt he'll want all his dynamite store for this job."

"But why?" asked Tim.

"Well," said the smith, rubbing his beard, "there's never been any stirring Mr. Threlby of Threlby End since his wife died. Folks tells of how, when she was alive, she came over here and spied around, and was fair mad for him to get going at some of them old cottages. It was said that something surely was going to happen at last. But she died, and nowt did happen."

"He's just a beastly old miser!" said Bob. "They say he works five acres of land round Threlby with one tottering old woman."

"And that he's sold all the charcoal-burning rights on Boarside to the Dennings Gunpowder Company," said Tim. "Birkett, the charcoal-burner, told us."

"'They say' is always a poor lass to talk after,"

said the smith cautiously. "There! Now, my lad, thoo's right!" And he let down Nimrod's hoof and smoothed the glossy chestnut foreleg.

"Some of it must be true," argued Nell; "and, anyhow, we are not going to be trampled upon by any old miser!"

The smith gave a big laugh.

"Well, I wish your father luck, miss, and so does a deal beside."

"But has it never struck you," said Roddy, with a suspicious solemnity, "that, if the scheme succeeds, we at The Warren will be stony broke? If no one is ever ill again—all modelled up, you know —then the poor doctor and his wife and kids will have to hook it to the next slum."

"There's no model village in this world as will put a stop to cranks," said Gregory. "There's always some folk with nowt the matter with 'em who'll want a doctor to kill 'em."

"I'll explain that to Dr. Webster," said Nell joyously.

A few minutes later the three were mounted. Nell rode astride in riding-breeches, gaiters, and a long brown holland coat.

"Go a bit careful now, Miss Nell," warned the smith, "until he gets the feel of his new shoe."

"Right oh!" called Nell gaily, and they trotted off with a most unusual sobriety.

CHAPTER VIII
The Old Abbey

MORLEY prided itself on being one of the highest and bleakest villages on the road to Scotland.

The main line from the south wound upwards at a steep gradient, and the expresses, with two engines, panted and groaned on their arduous way, until, just as they reached the quarries, they gave a snort of relief, and began the descent in a cheerful kind of hurry.

The village was an ancient one, but it had grown with the growth of the quarry industry, and it was certainly true that homes for the workers, their wives and families, were badly wanted.

East and west of the village, the fells stretched away in grim wildness, and in winter, when all the fells turned to a monstrous ocean of untamable snow — snow and vivid blue sky, or snow and moonlight and stars—it felt rather frightening.

But to-day the sun was shining fiercely on the dusty limestone road, and the three trotted for about a mile before they came to a sign-post.

As Nell was the lady, Nimrod was allowed to choose the direction, and he instantly showed his intelligence by turning to the left, due west, down a narrow lane with stone walls on each side.

Nimrod had a good reason for his choice, for the road which led down to the famous old Scald Abbey was a favourite one. The Abbey was in ruins, but the farm was a decidedly going concern, and Mrs. Masterman, the tenant, was a great personage in the farming world, and, having the utmost respect for the doctor, she always made the children heartily welcome.

The horses also knew the joys of the Abbey stables, for these were real stables, where there was no smell of insulting petrol, nor the sound of snorting cars to irritate their feelings.

"It's the Abbey! Good old Nimrod!" laughed Roddy, as the horse pulled his head obstinately round. "Come on, kids!"

"Yes, come on!" echoed Tim. "It's an awful time since we had any breakfast."

Roddy shook his bridle, and off they trotted at a good pace. Roddy was chuckling to himself, for he had absolutely made up his mind which way they were going. He was bent on finding out whether his champion really did live at Threlby End, but he was at present willing to keep up the pretence of letting the horses choose.

"Bother—my cap!" cried Nell, as it dropped far in the dust behind her.

Tim and she pulled up, and the boy flung his rein to her, dismounted, and ran back.

"Thanks awfully!" said Nell, as she took the cap from him, and began dashing off the dust against her coat. "I knew the elastic was groggy. Have you a pin?"

"You couldn't use a pin out riding if I had," he said. "Besides, I haven't one."

"All right, I'll manage," and she knotted the broken elastic into a loop and hung the cap round her arm.

"What's up?" called Roddy from some distance in front, as he rounded on his saddle.

"The usual," shouted Tim.

"Nell come to bits? Why do girls always come to bits?"

But the insult in this remark made Nell cry wildly: "Go for him, Nimrod!"

How they galloped! Nimrod's shoe had evidently been properly put on.

But presently it was necessary to slacken pace, for the road descended steeply, and an entrancing view greeted the adventurers.

Below them there ran a shallow trout stream, with broken patches of trees on either bank, while beyond the river the old Abbey ruins rose majestically from rich pasture lands, backgrounded by sweeping fells, warm with sunshine and colour.

They walked their horses carefully down the rough track, crossed the rude stone bridge, and, scorning the handsome dwelling which lay somewhat to their left, they rode into the farm-yard and into such a hullabaloo as could only take place at a sheep-shearing.

From far and wide over the fells the Abbey sheep had been gathered, and the lambs had been separated from the ewes by rough arrangements of hurdles.

Hence the appalling noise of baaing and bleating, and men's voices, and sharp barking of dogs. As the horses clattered over the stones, Mrs. Masterman herself appeared, looking very business-like in her dark-blue overall, as she bustled amongst the workers, seeing that everything was going right.

"Good morning, Mrs. Masterman," cried Roddy. He had reined up, and was off his horse in a jiffy.

"Bless the children! And what's the news? Quick! Before I faint!"

"Don't faint, please!" cried Nell. "There isn't any news."

"Saturday," suggested Tim.

"Don't you see, Mrs. Masterman," explained Nell, "we are out for adventure, and we let Nimrod choose first, and of course he chose the Abbey."

"I see." Mrs. Masterman's eyes could flash sternly, but they could twinkle also. Just now they twinkled. "Then I've only to thank Nimrod for this pleasure, eh?"

As there was no possible retort to this remark they laughed merrily, and as Tim and Nell dismounted, a farm man came up, and at a nod from his mistress he took the horses off to the stable.

"We'll be having 'drinkings' round directly," said their hostess genially. "That is likely what you came for, just as the horses came for the corn-bin."

"I do believe that you were born the wisest woman in the world," admitted Tim. His eyes could twinkle too.

"We must help in this job first," said Roddy. "Do let us have a shot with the shears!"

"Yes; we'll never learn younger," agreed Tim.

"And a fine talking-to I'd get from your mother next time she comes round if I let you get yourselves all over sheep-grease in those clothes!" said Mrs. Masterman.

"These clothes!" said Roddy scornfully, and they walked on with the mistress.

On the way to the shearing-shed they passed the lamb-dipping trough, and they stood to watch with immense interest as the lambs were forced one by one through a narrow passage, up an inclined plane, to the edge of a vat of sheep-dip. Here they were caught by the shepherd and plunged deep down into the strong-smelling liquid. In vain they struggled and gasped. They were soused thoroughly, and when released they scrambled off along another gangway out to their companions in distress.

But in the long shed a score of men were gathered, each sitting astride a low, sloping board, on which an unfortunate sheep lay prone on its back, with its legs tied, being shorn of its heavy winter coat.

The men worked with skill and great speed, and as the last strand of wool was clipped loose the cord was untied, and the sheep was pushed off the board, at which it scrambled right side up, and wandered off with a bewildered expression on its face. But its trials were not even yet over, for it was again caught by a couple of men who sat at a great cauldron of boiling tar, into which they plunged branding-irons, to brand all the newly-shorn sheep with a conspicuous M.

There was plenty of fun going on, for the Abbey shearing had brought together a throng of workers from the surrounding farms, all ready to help and to enjoy the shearing feast which was to be held later.

The girls raked up the loose wool, or brought refreshments in large enamel mugs to the shearers, or carried off the fleeces to a high barn, where the men adroitly turned them inside out and stacked them up in readiness for the wool-buyer.

Of course the children joined in the sport, and, as they were well known and popular, they were soon laughing and chaffing with everyone, and after enjoying mugs of tea and currant pasty the boys set to work to tug an obstreperous sheep to the shearing-bench.

But it isn't as easy to get a sheep to go your way as it looks, and while Roddy and Tim were exercising their muscles over a heavy old lady, who would try to bolt backwards to her crying lamb, Nell stood giggling hysterically at their efforts.

"Those clothes! Those clothes!" cried Mrs. Masterman. "I think I could find you a more useful occupation than to mess yourselves up like this!"

"Oh, what?" they cried. The boys released the sheep, and she instantly made a lumbering yet surprisingly active dodge backwards from the shed.

"Well, how would you all fancy riding over into Boardale to tell Birkett that I'm frantic for the pea-sticks he promised to send last week? Never again will I trust the faithful word of a man. What with the second crop of peas and the beans, we are desperate, and I haven't a man to spare."

"We'll go like a shot!" said Roddy, thinking that the stars in their courses were fighting for him in his own plot. Birkett's cottage was only ten minutes' walk from Threlby End.

"And mind you put it straight to Birkett," said Mrs. Masterman. "Tell him that to play fast and loose with a proper business woman is just cutting his own throat."

"Oh, we'll pile it on!" said Tim. "We'll tell him that, so long as the world lasts, Mrs. Masterman will never give him another order for a pea-stick unless——"

"We'll set Nell on!" interrupted Roddy. "She's going in for training in a course of Women's Rights. By the time she grows up, there won't be a man left in the world, who isn't grovelling at her feet."

"Don't beguile me into any more waste of time," laughed Mrs. Masterman, as she hurried away on further business.

The children were about to get their horses, when they were surprised by the appearance of a girl in a tweed costume, who was wearing a purple, green, and white ribbon in her hat, and a rosette with the same colours on her coat.

She carried a handbag, and strode boldly into their midst.

For a moment she gazed about her coolly, as though she were calculating her chances. Then she opened her bag and took out a packet of leaflets.

"Please, will you help me to distribute these?" she said, pouncing upon Nell.

"What are they?" she asked cautiously.

"They are about votes for women," she answered in a keen, joyous kind of a voice.

"Why, are you a real Suffragette from London?" asked Nell, flushing red with rosy excitement.

"Yes, from London. But I have heaps of friends in the north, and I want to find more."

"Come on, Nell!" said Bob under his breath. "We must go."

But Nell shook her head and pouted obstinately. She did not meet a real Suffragette from London every day.

"Have you been in prison?" she asked eagerly.

"Not yet," and the girl smiled radiantly. "But will you help me? I heard there was a great gathering here, so I came."

"To seek out all these down-trodden women?" asked Tim coolly, as he waved his hand towards the merry farm-girls.

He wore his most dangerously mild expression.

"Or to blow up something?" asked Nell yearningly.

"Just to distribute a little literature," said the stranger. "The masses want educating."

"I'd adore to help you!" said Nell, holding out her hand.

"Don't be an ass!" said Roddy, his brow darkening. "We can't waste all the morning like this."

"Well, you two can go. I am going to work for my sex," said Nell irritatingly.

The Suffragette gave a little laugh, and handed Nell a bunch of ribbons.

"Oh, thanks awfully!" cried Nell, as she pinned them into her coat.

The boys looked at each other and turned off in disgust. It was just like Nell to spoil their day. You never could depend on what she might take it into her head to do.

But Nell led the way into the shearing-shed, and the workers, looking up, grinned with some anticipation of fun.

"You all have to take these papers!" said Nell in her most ringing tone. "I don't care a bit whether you men hate us women or not, but we are going to get the vote—so there!"

Nell's challenge brought down a shout of laughter, and some of the women clapped their hands a little mockingly.

But the Suffragette, backing up the young spokeswoman, went from bench to bench, handing out her papers and chatting and arguing in the most delightful style, and in a few moments everyone was talking and arguing, and doing exactly what the Suffragette wanted.

"Why, all of you," and she turned to a group of bright-eyed young women, "do twice as much work as any man, and get half his wages."

"That's news!" grumped one of the shearers.

"It's true enough!" exclaimed a girl named Polly Dennison. "It's toil and slave for the women, and the menfolk like to rogue us out of every sixpence!"

"Thoo'll be getting thyself into jail, my lass, Polly," said one of the men with a grunt. "It's not so nice there as some females seems to think."

"Why, have you tried?" struck in Nell keenly.

There was a general laugh at the man's expense; but Roddy and Tim, who were wrathfully watching Nell and her new friend, began to plot together to leave her.

"Hobnobbing with a perfect stranger like that! It's disgusting!" said Tim.

"Aye, my lad," laughed one of the men. "Lads is out of it, sure enough, this time!"

But Nell was not quite so far gone as to wish really to miss her adventure-ride, and she came dancing up to the boys in a rather exasperating way, as she said challengingly:

"She is going to speak on Morley Green to-night, so we had better hurry up. I want to hear her."

"You can't. You promised to go to the Flower Show Meeting," snapped Roddy.

"That doesn't matter."

"Oh, go on! Break your word! Chuck your engagements! That is a woman all over!" sneered Tim.

"If you are going to be horrid I shan't come with you at all!" said Nell. "You are only mad because you think I shall be equal with you some day."

"Be equal now," said Tim. "Don't expect me to get off my horse and grovel in the dust for your cap. You can get it yourself next time."

"Silly!" said Nell aggravatingly. "I'll just go and wish her 'good-bye', and then I'll come."

The worst of it was that the boys considered themselves in charge of Nell, so that they could not relieve their feelings by cutting her, but it was certainly maddening to hear the way she was going on.

But when Nell returned and saw their glum faces she pulled herself together and exercised all her wiles to make them jolly again, and when Nell tried her best to be nice she was hard to resist.

But just as they were leaving the farm-yard Polly Dennison came running up.

"If you're going to Birkett's you'll likely be going Brow Side way, won't you?"

"Yes," said Roddy. "Anything we can do?"

"Only if you'd let my mother know that I'm stopping the night here, I'd be obliged."

"Right you are," answered Roddy. "Any particular reason?"

"Her young man, of course," struck in Tim.

Polly gave an awkward laugh.

"It's nowt of t' sort! It's only that I want to get to Morley and hear what yon young lady has to say for herself, and it would be overlate to get to Brow Side afterwards."

"It's a gay catching business, is this here Suffragetting," remarked a man who was leaning against the gate.

"It's catching because we are in the right," said Nell cheerfully.

CHAPTER IX

A Rest at Brow Side

THE three turned westwards, and took a steep track up the side of a mountain stream, aiming for the pass which led over into Boardale.

It was a very rough fell road, and the horses walked slowly with heads bent low.

"Bother the flies!" groaned Nell, as she slashed Nimrod's neck to right and left with a big bracken frond. "It is abominable for you to be devoured like this, you poor darling!"

Indeed, a pestering cloud of insects danced about each horse's neck, making them fidget incessantly.

But presently a fence crossed the fell from a wall to their right, reaching to the stream far below on their left.

Beyond this fence there were signs of life. Geese cropped the short turf and hens made dust-holes in the sunshine. Low mortarless walls surrounded a considerable orchard, while a little in advance there was a conspicuous group of pines and yews, planted to protect the farm from the driving winter gales.

The horses, having passed through the gate in

the fence, now turned round by a giant cedar between the orchard and the "planting", and after
picking their way over a road of sun-hardened ruts,
they clattered on to the paving-stones of a farm-
yard, to the accompaniment of the furious barking
of four dogs and the indignant screams of a long-
necked gander.

A tall, bony woman came out into the white-
washed porch and eyed the intruders discontentedly.

"You talk, Roddy. You have the sunny, allur-
ing smile," whispered Nell.

Roddy was usually put up as spokesman on difficult occasions, for he had a "way with him" which
got him what he wanted.

"Please, Mrs. Dennison," he said cheerfully,
"we have brought a message to you from your
daughter. She is stopping overnight in Morley,
and she asked us to let you know."

"Oh, did she?" demanded Mrs. Dennison with
terrific emphasis. "And did she happen to mention who was to do her work while she gads about
yonder?"

Roddy shook his head and wrinkled his forehead
thoughtfully.

"You explain," he said to Nell. "It's more in
your line."

"It's always the way!" grumbled Mrs. Dennison.
"Young 'uns likes to bide where there is a crowd,
while they leave the work to be done by them that's
growing old and ought to be slackening off."

"Oh," struck in Nell, "but really, Mrs. Dennison, it's awfully important! Miss Dennison is going

to hear a glorious girl talk about equal rights for
women, and I am going too."

"What?" Mrs. Dennison looked as if she could
stab Nell with her pointed nose. "Them Suffragettes hasn't landed in these parts, have they?"

"Rather. And I am a real one too;" and Nell
pointed to her ribbons.

"Well, if that doesn't cap all!" cried the worried
woman.

But Tim, sick of the vexed question, struck in:

"This must be an awfully lonely kind of place!
Doesn't the wind howl in those trees at night?"

"Aye, a bit; but there's no harm in t' wind.
It's company."

"Is it?" said Tim. He hadn't thought of it.

"I wonder, Mrs. Dennison," said Roddy,
"whether you would be so awfully kind as to let
us have some meal and water for the horses? We
are going to ride over into Boardale, and it is
thirsty work climbing your hill."

"Welcome enough," she answered. "T' bucket
is there for the handling, and t' meal is in the bin
yonder," and she pointed to the stable door. "But
there's no one to wait on you but yourselves."

"We generally wait on ourselves," said Roddy,
as he dismounted with a jerk.

"Now, you'll be twins likely?" asked Mrs. Dennison, eyeing them with more attention.

"So people think," said Roddy shrugging his
shoulders. "But we aren't really. I'm the eldest
and the nicest—he's no good!"

"I had twins once," said Mrs. Dennison, as

though she had not heard the bantering remark.
"Polly and her brother; but what is a farm without
a lad of one's own?"

By this the children gathered that Polly's twin
brother had died, but they did not like to ask.

Nell slid down from her horse, and waited as the
boys went off to get the meal.

"Is there anything we can do to help you?" she
suggested; "we've lots of time, so long as we get
over into Boardale this afternoon."

"You'll have to do a bit of careful riding," said
the woman. "There's not many folks bothers
with yon road nowadays, and it's getten terr'ble
rough."

"Couldn't we fetch in the cows or something?"
pleaded Nell.

A ray of cheerfulness crossed the tired woman's
face.

"Well, I won't say but what I've worrited about
t' cows," she admitted. "Our farm lad would take
'em into the far intake, and then he went off to
Morley, and goodness only knows when he'll clear
himself out of t' 'Fox and Hounds'! And now
here's Polly gadding; and folk can't tell whether
they are on their head or their heels! I've a lot
of spring chickens wanting feeding down by the
beck as well, and my knees that swelled with rheumatics that——"

"We'll do everything," cried Nell. "I'll feed
the chickens, and the boys shall go for the cows."

Tim was working hard at the pump handle, while
Roddy was mixing the meal with a piece of stick.

"Boys!" said Nell, frowning at them meaningly. "Mrs. Dennison will be awfully glad if you would bring down the cows from the high intake. I'm going to feed the chickens."

"All right!" said Roddy easily. "We can milk them too, if you like, Mrs. Dennison. We two can milk against a dozen!"

"I couldn't," said Nell. "Milking is so—so slippery sort of!"

"Happen not brought up to it, my lass," she said. "But I can manage t' milking grand. It's getting about on t' fell that gives my knees such 'what for'."

While the boys went for the cows, Nell made herself completely at home. She spied into the dairy, and examined the old oak in the kitchen, and was especially interested in some big hooks which hung from the ceiling close behind the wide entrance door.

"Them's not been used for many a long day," said her hostess, "except for an odd ham now and again. They were set there for lifting off the loads from the pack-horses."

"Why, is this a pack-horse route?" asked Nell.

"Aye; not fifty years ago the pack-horses came right over here from Boardale way, many a dozen of them every week, and they stopped at Brow Side to rest before they went on past the Abbey to Morley and away far enough. They carried everything from a pint-pot to a wincey petticoat!"

Mrs. Dennison was stooping over the fire, pulling down the kettle and piling on some sticks.

"You'll have to stop for a bite of summut," she said. "I don't ken you, but an hour's job gets an hour's meat, and you'll not find much on t' road from here to Boardale."

"It's awfully good of you," said Nell gratefully. "I'm Mr. M'Leod's daughter, of the Quarries, you know; and the boys are Dr. Webster's terrors!"

"Never Dr. Webster of Morley?"

Nell nodded, and was surprised to see Mrs. Dennison's cheeks flush.

"Well—I never did! It was Dr. Webster who came and saw the last of poor Fred. He came up here one snowy night, up to his knees in snow, but never a grumble! I'll not forget that in a hurry. He stayed all night, till my lad died, and my husband had not been dead a year!"

"How awful!" said Nell sympathetically. "It isn't nice to see your mother die, you know. I was ten when my mother died, but they let me stay. She slept herself away into Heaven, and left me here."

"Trouble comes as trouble will," said the woman mournfully; "and they say that God Almighty knows best, but it comes hard!"

They were interrupted by the sounds of barking dogs, shouting boys, mooing cows, and when at last the boys had completed their work, and Nell had fed the chickens, they were all quite pleased to sit down to their third meal that day at Mrs. Dennison's bountifully spread table, and by the way they chattered anyone would have imagined that they had known their hostess all their lives.

But a little later, when Nell shyly asked Mrs. Dennison what they owed for their meal, she gave them quite a cheerful laugh.

"Bless me! Think I would take anything from Dr. Webster's lads! What, you've all served for your bit!"

"It's the first time we've been out to real farm service in our lives," said Roddy.

"Pity but what you were 'stoppin' on '," said Mrs. Dennison.

"We mustn't take on another job until we have finished the one in hand," said Tim. "We don't want to get into a row with Mrs. Masterman. It's a jolly good way over into Boardale, and I think we ought to be on the go!"

CHAPTER X

A Forgotten Birthday

KITTY'S exam was over, and she was quite certain
that she had failed. She hadn't a vestige of hope,
and yet the suspense was unendurable. It was the
mathematics that had floored her, for she had been
as nervous as a cat on ice when she went into the
examination-room, and, having read through the
paper, she simply couldn't concentrate on any one
question, but jumped from one to another, getting
more nervy every time she looked at the clock.

Uncle Jonathan had gone off to London—of all
extraordinary things to do. He had left on the
Monday morning, and to-day was Saturday, and
he might or might not return this evening—Marjory didn't know.

"Let's go up Boar Fell and celebrate the failure,
Don," said Kitty bitterly, for she was in one of her
lowest moods.

She had so set her heart on this scholarship,
which would have admitted her, with every expense
paid, to the Northport Training College for Girls,
which was handsomely endowed by a wealthy
Liverpool cotton-broker.

"Of course I know that if I had got in I should

only have been a kind of a charity girl," Kitty thought miserably, "but I would rather take charity from a stranger in Liverpool than from Uncle Jonathan. However, Don boy, I'm just a wretched failure, and I shall have to go out into the streets with my fiddle or ride bareback for a living after all!"

Kitty went at a mad gallop down the drive with Don at her heels, but on reaching the road she crossed it, and, turning somewhat to the right, she passed over a quaint footbridge which spanned a wide and shallow stream which had its birthplace up amongst the mossy wildernesses of Boar Fell.

Kitty dearly loved Boar Fell. It was not outstandingly high, but it rose in a long, wild sweep, deeply cut towards the centre by the beck.

For there were times when the lazy, shallow stream roared and swelled and impudently overleaped all boundary, as it swept a fell-load of snows and drenching rains into the valley.

At first Kitty had been afraid of the lonely fell, and it was Don who had taught her that there was nothing to fear, because every inch of the ground was exciting to his busy nose. The ancient pack-horse track could still be traced, and Marjory told a weird story of how a pack-horse and his driver had once walked upwards into the mist and had never been heard of again, except when a stray shepherd, belated on some winter afternoon, heard the clicking of the hoofs and even saw a giant horse and driver through the gloom.

Birkett, who cut wood for the coaling or char-

coal burning, had warned Kitty that she must
never go up Boar Fell when the mist hung low and
the dogs howled.

But on this glorious afternoon the fell was rich
in colour, and looked exactly as if it were longing
to break into gay laughter.

"You don't know, you great foolish thing, that
I have failed in that disgusting exam!" said Kitty
grimly. "You would never dare to look so jolly
if you knew that."

Then her brow clouded worse than before.
"Perhaps you want to make it up to me because it
is my birthday to-day. Nobody knows it is my
birthday, nobody in all the wide world!"

She strode onward with a light, swinging pace,
not troubling to keep the track, but leaping lightly
from tussock to tussock of reedy grass or over low
mounds of heather not yet come to bloom.

Reaching higher ground, the bright green bil-
berry bushes shone out brilliantly. Once a small
bird flew upwards, startled at her footfall. She
stooped and, searching, counted five chocolate-
mottled eggs, warm from the life inside them.

Don watched her with slowly moving tail as she
kneeled, but she shook her head warningly at him,
and he reluctantly understood that the find had
nothing to do with him.

The sun was still very hot, even though well
turned on his western way down the great blue
heavens, which were lightened in the east by a thin
lacy veil of cloud.

Kitty had no intention of really mounting the

pass. She was tired and limp, but she did wish to escape from the house that she might think; so, climbing a few paces beyond the nest, she flung herself down that she might watch for the bird's return.

Yet what was there to think about, except that it was her birthday, and that her mother was not there to kiss her and give her some wonderful surprise? Yet if she turned from her birthday she was forced to think of the horrible humiliation before her, when she would have to admit to Uncle Jonathan, when the lists came out, that she had failed!

" I'd just like to run right away over that pass and chance finding my fortune out in the wide world!" she thought desperately. But, knowing quite well that she was being silly, she flung herself backwards and closed her eyes sleepily.

She was suddenly roused from a genuine little nap by a low growl from Don.

He had lifted himself up on his fore paws, and was looking towards the head of the pass, where the sky dropped down like a brilliant blue wedge in between the two breasts of the fell.

Horses!

Kitty leaped up as though transfixed.

Only half awake, they seemed to her like something in a dream.

But no! There were three horses, ridden by two boys and a girl, and their gay voices could be heard through the breathless air, as they hallooed and cooed across the dale.

What impudent intruders they were! And yet

Kitty could forgive them anything so long as they brought horses within sight of her longing eyes.

They were coming zigzag fashion down the track, very slowly, for the horses' hoofs slipped continually on the loose rain-washed stones. As they descended, Kitty could see that they were all capless, and that the girl in front had a mass of springy golden hair tied up behind. The young life conquering the age-old fell made a pretty picture, and as they reached a stretch of more level ground, the girl, shaking her reins, began to trot.

"You idiot, Nell!" shouted one of the boys.

"Come on, it's all right now!" rang out the girl's voice.

"She's mad!" exclaimed Kitty. Don and she stood watching breathlessly.

That the horse should keep his feet at that pace and on that ground was a miracle. The girl must be mad!

Perhaps Nell realized her folly. At any rate she drew in her rein with a sudden nervousness.

"Oh!" Kitty sprang forward and ran a hundred yards at top speed.

Nimrod had stumbled badly, come down on both knees, and shot his rider over his head. Poor Nell lay twisted up on the rocky track.

Kitty had her arm about her in a few moments, and the boys, leaping off their horses, let them go as they would.

Nell uttered a groan and clutched hard at Kitty's hand.

"I am afraid you are hurt," said Kitty anxiously.

"Yes." Nell tried to raise herself, and then sank back with a cry. The pain was sickening.

"Is Nimrod hurt?" she gasped.

No one was thinking of Nimrod, but Roddy could see the ominous red trickling down his forelegs. He had scrambled up, and was looking at his fallen mistress with wonder in his large intelligent eyes, as he trembled from head to foot.

"Oh, he's all right!" said Tim lightly.

"I've let him down, the darling!" cried Nell, with a queer hysterical gulp. "Oh!"

She sank back with a shriek of pain, and as Kitty held her fast she closed her eyes and fainted away.

The boys stared speechlessly at Kitty.

"Get some water, quick!" she commanded. Both boys rushed, and Kitty undid Nell's blouse, laid her head back, and began to fan her violently with her handkerchief.

The boys came dashing back, carrying two dripping caps, and what little water was left was poured over Nell's face, and in a few moments, to their unspeakable relief, she opened her eyes and tried to move.

"Lie still!" said Kitty authoritatively. "You will soon be all right."

"Shall I? Oh, don't touch my arm, please!"

"Dislocated her shoulder, I bet," said Tim with professional interest. He stooped and tried very gently to move Nell's right arm.

"Oh, don't!" she wailed.

"That's it!" said Tim, nodding his head sagely.

Tim haunted his father's surgery, where, every now and then, when his mother was out, and his father needed an extra hand, he was allowed the bliss of assisting. Recently he had been acting as a model for an ambulance class amongst the quarrymen, and had openly longed for a real accident to test his knowledge.

"You'll be all right, Nell," he said, gently enough. "It's not dangerous, but only beastly painful!"

"But what ought we to do?" asked Kitty. Tim spoke with such confidence that somehow she found herself bowing to his authority.

"It will hurt her frightfully when we lift her," he said under his breath, "but we must tie her up somehow and get her down from here."

"She must come to our house," said Kitty, "and then we must send for a doctor."

"The doctor will be Father," said Tim. "Is your house far?"

"Threlby End. You can see it through the trees."

"O—oh!" He darted a queer look at Kitty which she did not understand, but Roddy, listening, felt that he had gained the object of the expedition. They had discovered that his champion lived at Threlby End.

"Oh, Roddy!" called Nell. "Tell me truly. Have I killed Nimrod?"

"Rather not!" stammered he. "Nimrod is all right. I mean he is eating grass," for he had pulled him away out of sight of his mistress.

"But go and make sure."

Now Roddy had gone nearly as green as sea-weed through sympathy with Nell, so he turned off with relief to stroke down Nimrod's forelegs and examine the extent of the damage.

"Sickening!" he murmured. "Stones under the mossy road. Why did she do it? I always knew that——"

But what was the earthly good of thinking "I told you so!" when the deed was done?

"Poor old man!" he whispered, as he soothed the trembling animal and led him off towards the stream, that he might bathe the wounds.

But meanwhile Tim was taking upon himself to act as he imagined his father would have acted under the circumstances.

"You must buck up, Nell!" he said with a grown-up firmness. "You will have to let us tie you up a bit. We will hurt you as little as we can."

"Shall I tear up my petticoat?" asked Kitty quickly.

"No, we'll manage. Roddy," he shouted, "hand over your stockings."

Roddy was down on the ground in a moment undoing his shoes, and leaving Nimrod he came racing back and handed his stockings to Tim.

"You just hurry up and take the horses down to Threlby, and then ride off for Father," said the young commander.

"And Daddy too, please," put in Nell. Her lip was trembling ominously.

"And Mr. M'Leod, of course," said Tim. Then,

having given his orders, he tied his own and Roddy's stockings together, and directed Kitty how to help him to tie Nell's arm to her side.

"Oh, don't!" pleaded Nell.

"We must! We can't have it jogging! It's swelling up like anything, and we must get you off to bed as soon as ever we can!"

"Can we carry her?" asked Kitty. "I'm awfully strong."

"We must try," said Tim. Even the enthusiastic Tim did not quite fancy the job of moving his patient under such torturing circumstances. But at last they managed to raise her to her feet, and, finding that she could stand, they joined hands and managed to seat her between them.

"Put your left arm round Katherine Threlby's neck!" said Tim, and he gave an irresistible wink at the new friend. Kitty smiled at him, for she also had recognized the three.

Unluckily, just at that moment Roddy passed with the horses, and Nell caught a glimpse of Nimrod's knees.

Her fortitude gave way with a burst, and she began to sob hysterically.

"Put me down," she wailed. "Let me see Nimrod."

"Hurry off, Roddy!" ordered Tim.

"And please," put in Kitty, "if you see our housekeeper, Marjory, tell her to get ready my bed."

"All right!" said Roddy, and he led the horses away.

"Nell, you are not to be ridiculous!" scolded Tim. "Slow march, please!" and he frowned at Kitty.

But the motion, gentle as it was, hurt poor Nell horribly.

"I can't bear it! I can't!" she stormed.

"Go on!" said Tim to Kitty.

And for ten awful minutes Nell had to bear it.

CHAPTER XI

The Best they Can

RODDY always gave way to Tim when anything medical was the matter, for accidents to people always made him feel sick; but with animals he was bold enough, and kind with a true animal-lover's kindness.

As he walked up the drive he took stock of the place with the keenest interest. How often he and Tim had wished to see what lay behind that yew hedge!

But there was no time to examine anything properly, and as he clattered into the yard with his three horses Marjory came out to meet him.

"There has been an accident," he said bluntly. "The others are bringing her down; and please, may I leave these horses in your stable while I gallop off for my father—Dr. Webster, you know?"

"Why, certainly!" cried Marjory. "But who is hurt? Will the lady want a bed?"

"Yes. Katherine Threlby said I was to tell you to get her bed ready. It is Nell M'Leod who is hurt. And could you ask one of your men to see to this horse—bathing—that kind of thing?

He's worth a lot, and it's rotten luck; but a girl comes before a horse, so I must go."

Roddy saw his invalid and Hop into the stable, then, flinging himself on Rufus, he trotted off, and broke into a reckless gallop as soon as he gained the main road.

"One of the men, indeed!" thought Marjory to herself. "Samuel is off for the week-end. However, as the young gentleman said, a girl comes before a horse," and she rushed off to get ready the room.

She had only just finished when Kitty and Tim came staggering into the yard, carrying Nell, who was almost in a state of collapse.

Marjory lifted Nell clean out of the arms of the exhausted young people, and, carrying her upstairs, she laid her down on Kitty's bed.

Nell, too weak to make any resistance, gave a feeble groan and then lay quite still.

"Can't we do anything until the doctor comes?" asked Kitty.

"Yes, hot bottles," said Marjory, as she felt Nell's cold clammy hands.

They flew to get hot bottles, and hot blankets, and hot milk, and Tim fetched and carried like any woman, making himself completely at home in the strange house. At last a sense of ease overcame Nell, and to the surprise of her anxious attendants she fell into a light sleep.

"That's luck!" said Tim critically. "Let's hope she sleeps until Father comes. He will give her a whiff of chloroform and straighten her up."

"I'll watch her, if you two like to go down-stairs," said Marjory. "Get the young gentleman some tea, Miss Kitty!"

"Yes, come!" said Kitty, and she took Tim off, down the narrow stairs and along the flagged passage to the old kitchen.

Tim had now time to look round and consider things, and he could not help being surprised at being brought into the kitchen for his meal. He was too polite to say anything, and indeed he thought the girl was going to put on the kettle and go into some other room afterwards.

As he stood rather uncertainly at the door, Kitty looked across at him whimsically and gave a merry laugh.

"I don't even know your name," she said.

"I'm Tim. The rest of it is 'othy', but we never mention it. I once saw you in a train, and I saw you lick the others at jumping, and I watched you swotting at arithmetic—and you counted on your fingers."

"That's me!" admitted Kitty. She hadn't spoken to a boy for ages and ages, and there was something in Tim that appealed to her.

"Are you by any chance a medical student?" she asked mischievously.

"You've hit it! Been serving my apprenticeship ever since I pulled out Roddy's first tooth. Roddy is the other one, you know—Roderick Morrison Webster, when he's all there."

"Really!" said Kitty.

"People think we are twins. But we aren't.

I'm a year younger than Roddy, but I caught him
up."

"A kind of Jacob?"

"Tweedledee!"

"Oh, but he was the nasty one!" said Kitty.
"He spoiled the nice new rattle.   But please sit
down in that rocking-chair.   It is quite comfy.
Do you like home-made scones?"

"Dote on them," said Tim.   "Only, if you don't
mind, I'd just like to have a look at Nimrod.   Nell
will absolutely turn into a maniac if there is anything really wrong with him.   Of course it was all
her own fault."

"That doesn't make it any easier," pronounced
Kitty.

"So you've found that out?" asked Tim, with a
little shrug of one shoulder.

"It comes with age," said Kitty, drawing herself up.   "But—yes, let's go out to Nimrod—the
stable is only across the yard."

"I'd like to see that your man is doing him all
right," said Tim as they went out together.

"We have no proper coachman," said Kitty,
"and our one-and-only is off for the week-end.
When things want doing here we generally do
them."

"Oh!" Tim did not quite know how to take this
last remark.

"Empty, swept, and garnished!" he thought as
he entered the stable and found Nimrod and Hop
standing in the empty stalls, with not so much as
a wisp of hay in the racks.

They turned and looked at him reproachfully for having brought them into such an empty land.

But Kitty pushed past him and went down on her knees to examine poor Nimrod's wounds.

"Poor old man!" she cried affectionately; "you ought to be walking off to the vet before your knees get stiff. But we must do something."

"Why, do you know about horses?" asked Tim.

"Everything," said Kitty vaguely.

She ran back to the house and brought out some clean rags, which she smeared over with a whole pot of her best cold cream, and she and Tim managed to bandage the injured knees quite respectably.

Then Kitty, joyful indeed at having come into touch with a real live horse once more, took Tim back into the kitchen and busily got the tea ready.

Now Tim was supposed to be rather stand-offish with visitors, while Roddy was labelled the "jolly one"; but when Tim was quite on his own he could be very good company.

Just now he was feeling rather inflated with a sense of his own importance, and he could not sit down to Kitty's generously spread meal until he had been upstairs again, to satisfy himself about the patient.

"She is sleeping beautifully!" said Marjory as Tim poked his head round the door.

"I hope Father hurries. But he may be miles and miles away—no one ever knows. We have many a goose-chase after him." And away he went back to the kitchen.

"Shall I call you Miss Threlby?" asked Tim as he swung the rocking-chair recklessly.

"I wouldn't. Kitty is good enough."

"Kitty! That's better. Katherine is rather——"

"Yes, isn't it?" laughed Kitty happily. She made up her mind to let herself go and have a proper birthday tea with this jolly boy.

"Yes; only, shall I tell you what we really call you?"

"If it isn't rude."

"Roddy's Champion. He bagged you as his favourite at the gym display, and he was frightfully cocky that you turned out the winner."

"I could always jump. That was nothing."

"It was jolly good!" asserted Tim, just a trifle patronizingly. "You know, it's funny how you never really do know people until you do know them, isn't it?"

"How do you mean?" Kitty was not yet used to Tim's style.

"Well"—the boy carefully balanced a heavy load of greengage jam on his bread and butter— "we couldn't quite make out what kind you really were. Sometimes you laughed, and sometimes— you looked as if your mouth was stuck for ever! In the train, now, you know, you knew who we were, and you must have guessed that we wanted to be jolly, and yet you wouldn't."

"I wasn't in the mood," admitted Kitty.

"Grumps?" enquired Tim calmly. "People make such a rumpus when one grumps, but the fact is, it's the only thing to do sometimes, isn't it?"

"The girls call me Kitty Up - and - Down," laughed Kitty. "They say they never know how they will find me."

Now, how did it happen that fifteen-year-old Kitty suddenly felt as though she would like to talk to this merry black-eyed boy about what was on her mind? Was it because she had found out that he understood all about the art of grumping?

"Have you ever been in for an exam?" she blurted out. "A big one I mean?"

"Not yet. They'll come all in good time, like rheumatics and death and that sort of thing!" said Tim serenely. "Have you?"

"Yes, and I've failed."

"Lists just out?"

"Not yet. But I am sure. Arithmetic! There isn't really time to use your fingers in an exam."

"While there is life there is hope," said Tim encouragingly. "Was it anything you cared about?"

"Yes, a scholarship."

"Ah!" Tim frowned. "Roddy and I go up for our shots in August. Doctors can't afford public schools for two at once. Too many clothes and side-shows and things! I don't see why one need go to a public school. I know a chap who never learnt a thing, and brought home nothing but cups and blazers, and his mother had to pay a frightful sum afterwards to a coach to get him squeaked through for a potty little business he wanted. But for you, why do you have to bother about scholarships and things?"

Now Tim was certainly longing to find out whether Kitty was really a relative of Mr. Threlby's, and, if so, why she was living in his kitchen. Perhaps it was just a chance that her name was Threlby.

"I think that is rather a fishing question," laughed Kitty. "You want to find out why I am giving you tea in the kitchen, instead of in the best drawing-room?"

Tim answered her with a long-drawn-out wink.

"You must be a witch, so you had better tell me."

"We are spring-cleaning."

"That is a girl's fib! Nobody spring-cleans in June."

"As you are so clever, do you know what a poor relation is?" asked Kitty in a harder tone.

"You don't mean that Mr. Threlby is a beast to you and keeps you in the background like Cinderella?" Tim's imagination was taking fire. Was Roddy's champion turning out to be an oppressed maiden waiting to be rescued from a cruel fate?"

"Do I look like Cinderella?"

"You are dark—Cinderella was dark—and if you were dressed up you would make a ripping princess!"

"No godmother, no pumpkin, and not even any rats. Don kills them all!"

Don stirred at the word "rats", and poked his nose upwards to lick his mistress's hand.

"Why don't you get Mr. Threlby to lend you some of the family jewels and dress up?" asked

Tim. "You should see Nell when she has the dressing-up fit on her!"

But Kitty shook her head.

"My uncle would have a fit if I asked him such a thing."

So Mr. Threlby was her uncle. Tim had found out something.

"Well, how much pocket-money do you get?"

"Oh, as much as I want!" said Kitty, flushing. It suddenly struck her that it would be dishonourable to give away her uncle before a mere stranger boy.

Tim felt the snub, and anxious to prove that he hadn't asked for more information than he was willing to offer, he went on: "I get sixpence a week, but it goes nowhere! Don't you die for piles of money? My mother says that money is nothing, and that character is everything. But money is jolly convenient, and, as we haven't a soul in our family to leave us anything, we shall have to make it all ourselves!"

"And how are you going to make it?"

"Surgery! I shall invent some new operation and set the fashion. Appendicitis is getting played out. Why, even in our village six people have had it. Roddy has had it, and he has the most lovely scars. But my father wouldn't let me be done, though I made up a horrible pain. Can you sharpen your pencil with your left hand?"

"I can't even use my hanky with my left hand," laughed Kitty.

Tim shook his head solemnly.

"Fatal! You should learn. You never know how you might get stuck. I'm going in for being an ambidextrous surgeon. I shall live in Harley Street, London, and royalty and lord mayors and dotty old colonels will simply tumble over each other on my doorstep. I shall have a tremendous footman to let in my patients, and a nurse in uniform ready to help me."

"I think I had better train to be the nurse. Won't you have something more to eat?"

"Not a bite. This is my fourth meal to-day. I say! I wonder if it is beastly of us to be enjoying ourselves when Nell is so bad?"

"I don't see how it can hurt your sister——"

"Nell isn't our sister! She's an odd job. One by herself."

"So am I," struck in Kitty.

Tim chuckled.

"But Nell is worse than an odd job. She's turned into a raging Suffragette. She has really! She would burn down a barn as soon as look— and all because Roddy and I ragged her."

"It's dangerous to rag women," said Kitty solemnly.

"Too late to repent," sighed Tim. "Poor old Nell! She wanted to hear a real Suffragette speechify on Morley Green to-night. That will be U P!"

"I think—isn't that a car coming?" exclaimed Kitty, springing up.

Tim listened intently.

"My father's hoot. Know it in Timbuctu. Which way will it come?"

"Front door. Come along!"

Kitty led Tim down a long passage and through a door into an oak-wainscoted hall. The place looked gloomy indeed, even when she had pulled aside the blind. Then, unbarring the big door, she turned the key with both hands, and opened the door with a jerk.

To Tim the whole place smelt rather fusty; but he hadn't much time for thought, for the car was giving its last snort as he and Kitty stood on the steps.

Dr. Webster was there, so was Mr. M'Leod, so was a district nurse, so was Roddy.

"How is she?" demanded Mr. M'Leod as he flung open the door and leaped out.

"Asleep," said Tim. "This is Kitty. She invited us here."

"It was very good of you," said Nell's father, who was all on a nervous fidget to get to his daughter.

"I hope she will be all right," said Kitty shyly to the doctor. "We have done what we could."

"I am sure you have," said Dr. Webster genially. "Take me straight to her."

Kitty turned, and led the way up some wide oak stairs, along a gallery, through a green-baize door, along another corridor, until they reached, by a new route, the room where Nell was lying.

Roddy whispered to Tim that he had come back to take Nimrod off to the vet's, and he wanted his brother to come with him; but Tim frowned a violent "No!" and rushed after the others.

"Please, Father," he whispered, as he pressed close to him, "may I come in and see you operate?"

"Nonsense, Tim," said his father; "operation indeed!"

"When you poke the shoulder in, then?" he pleaded. "I faithfully promise that I won't stir nor make a sound."

"Don't worry me, Tim," said his father, and the budding surgeon turned away to plan his plan.

Marjory rose as Mr. M'Leod, the doctor, and the nurse came into the room.

Nell lay very still, breathing restlessly. Her face was pale, her hair lay all disordered, and she was still in her riding-coat, for they had not dared to try to get her arm out of the sleeve.

The doctor turned back the bed-clothes, and gave a smile as he noticed the first-aid bandaging.

"Tim," he murmured.

"She looks terribly white. May I speak to her?" whispered Mr. M'Leod as he leaned over his daughter.

"Please don't rouse her until I have found out whether Tim is right about the shoulder," he answered softly. "Nurse, I'll have this sleeve ripped up, please."

The district nurse stepped forward, and Marjory stood ready to help, thankful that the responsibility was off her shoulders.

But when Dr. Webster tried to move the swollen arm, Nell waked with a groan.

"Nell! My little girl!" said her father, and he kissed her tenderly on her forehead.

"Daddy! You've come!"

"Yes, darling child."

"Do see if Nimrod ought to be shot." Then she gave a heart-rending wail and shut her eyes very tight.

"You had better leave us for a little, M'Leod," the doctor ordered. "Let me manage with the women," and he looked towards Marjory and the nurse. "I shall soon find out what is wrong."

And so he did, for a few minutes later he came out on the landing and found Kitty seated on an old-fashioned window-seat, with Tim on one side of her and Mr. M'Leod on the other. How anxiously they waited for the verdict!

Kitty jumped up impulsively.

"How is she really?"

"Her shoulder is dislocated, and I shall have to administer chloroform before I can put it right. But as it would be both painful and exhausting to try to get her home, I wonder whether we may trespass a little further on your hospitality. She ought to stay where she is, that is the fact. Nurse would be left in charge."

"Of course she must stay," said Kitty earnestly. "My uncle would only be too pleased."

Dr. Webster was not certain about Mr. Threlby's pleasure, but he never cared a rap about anything outside the good of a patient.

"Then we will start at once," he said; "and if

you will help your maid to get a few things we want, I shall be greatly obliged."

"It is very good of you," exclaimed Mr. M'Leod anxiously.

"Oh no, it isn't! It isn't really! I love it!" said Kitty, hardly knowing what she said.

Then, keen to be of use, she rushed off and helped Marjory to get everything that the nurse needed.

But when all was ready, Kitty left the patient's room and found poor Nell's father waiting patiently.

"Are they going to begin?" he whispered.

"Yes," said Kitty sympathizingly. "And, please, don't you think you had better come downstairs?"

It was growing dark, for it was now about nine o'clock, and Nell's father could not see the speaker clearly.

"I would rather stay here," he said firmly. "My daughter might need me."

"That is what real fathers feel for their daughters," thought Kitty wistfully.

But Tim, seeing his chance, poked his face round the bedroom door.

"Father, mayn't I?"

But Dr. Webster was too occupied to notice his boy, so Tim crept into the room.

But meanwhile Roddy had escaped to the stable to examine the damage to Nimrod. It would be a relief, from thinking of what his father was doing to Nell, to attend to the suffering animal.

He stooped to feel down the horse's legs, and as

it was quite too dark to see clearly, he brought him out into the stable-yard and walked him up and down.

"They've managed to bandage him up a bit," he thought. "And he isn't actually lame. Oh, you daft old stumbler!" and he patted the horse affectionately. "You've been down, and your beauty is gone for ever, unless——"

His meditations were cut short by a terrible cry which rang forth from an upper window.

Roddy stood stock-still, and the perspiration beaded on his brow.

"What a fool I am!" he thought. "I know she is under chloroform. Tim is worth two of me. I guess he has sneaked into the room and is thoroughly enjoying himself. I had best take myself off with Nimrod as fast as the poor beast can walk."

CHAPTER XII

Mr. Threlby Hears Horses' Hoofs

"GRAND night, sir," said the station-master.

"Grand," said Mr. Threlby absently.

He had travelled from London, and it was a relief to leave the stifling train and feel the soft air blowing on his face.

Yet was he glad or sorry to be tramping that three miles to the home of his childhood? He hardly knew himself.

Mr. Threlby was physically strong, in the full vigour of middle life, and he walked fast, carrying his heavy bag as though he did not feel it.

When he reached Threlby End he knew that he would find Kitty. Yet, just because of an amazing letter he had received a week ago, he knew that he really did not want to see Kitty. He was afraid of her.

When he had taken the fourteen-year-old girl into his home a year ago he had thought that she was fatherless, motherless, and penniless. Yet now he had learned that she had not been fatherless, and that now she was very rich.

It might seem as though it would be an easy thing to tell a young girl that she was rich; but

though Mr. Threlby had not learnt to know Kitty
well, even he could guess that what he had to tell
her would hurt her in the very tenderest part of her
nature.

Kitty had evidently adored her dead father, and
had looked upon him as a great hero, who had
sacrificed himself for his queen and country in the
Boer War. Yet now it was his duty to tell his
niece that her father had not been a true hero at
all, and she would hate him worse than ever.

But did Kitty really hate him? Mr. Threlby was
never quite sure. Sometimes she was as gay and
jolly as though she had not a care in the world,
and sometimes she was so dull and grumpy that
he could not get a pleasant word out of her.

If only Kitty's Aunt Molly had lived! But, alas!
Mrs. Threlby had been killed across a fence—thrown
from her horse many years ago—and since her
death all the brightness and happiness had fled
away from the old hall.

Mr. Threlby knew that he had lived a coward's
life in selfishly nursing his grief. He had shrunk
from his friends and neighbours, and had shut up
most of the house—partly because he really was
much poorer than anybody knew, and partly because he liked to mope in solitude.

But as Mr. Threlby strode along he was not
thinking about his wife but about his brother,
Kitty's father.

Robert Threlby had always been from boyhood
careless and selfish, and bent on his own pleasure,
whatever it cost to others. As a man he was the

same, willing to do whatever happened to please himself, however he hurt others.

He managed to spend money like water, and always seemed to think that his elder brother ought to give him whatever he wanted, and over and over again Mr. Threlby had paid up his debts, and handed over large sums of money to save the family name from disgrace.

But one day the news came to him that Robert had actually married a girl who rode in a circus!

This was so dreadful to him that he never tried to find out whether a girl who rode in a circus might not be sweet and gentle and good.

Yet Kitty's mother was all this; and it was only through a tale of misfortune that the keen young Irish horsewoman had tried to earn her living by horsemanship in the ring.

But to Mr. Threlby she was nothing but a common circus-girl, and though he still continued to give his brother money, he made up his mind that he would never have anything to do with his wife.

Then the Boer War came, and his brother wrote asking him for another large sum to pay up his debts before he went out as a volunteer.

Again Mr. Threlby found the money, and shortly afterwards he read his brother's name in the list of the killed. Naturally he gave up the money he had lent as lost, and never troubled to find out what had become of his sister-in-law, while, as for Kitty, he did not even know that his brother had had a daughter.

So it had been a great shock to him when he had

received the last pathetic letter from Kitty's mother, pleading with him to take pity on her daughter. It had worried him dreadfully to be forced to upset his dull, retired life, even though he had never had a doubt but that it was his duty to offer Kitty a home.

When Kitty arrived with Marjory he had been shocked to find that she was the living image of her scapegrace father, and a dreadful horror seized him that perhaps when she grew up she also would be careless and extravagant and selfish, and would think that money did not matter so long as she enjoyed herself.

But unfortunately Mr. Threlby had, through his own fault, never learnt to know the sweet mother who had tried to put truer ideas of the meaning of life into Kitty's heart.

He had therefore kept her without money, under the foolish idea that somehow this would prevent her from falling into the very temptation which had ruined her poor father. But Mr. Threlby never guessed how lonely Kitty was, nor how she longed for pretty clothes and jolly times in the dreary old house.

Yet now, how was he to tell Kitty the news he had just heard?

Through a strange mistake, her father had not been killed in the Boer War, but had stayed all these years out in South Africa, without ever once writing to his wife. He had made a pile of money in mines, and had died about three months ago.

Mr. Threlby had heard everything from the lawyer in London, and it was clear enough to him that he must tell Kitty. How would she take it?

No wonder he was so absorbed in thought that he was quite startled at the sound of a sharp, whining voice.

"Oh, aye, Squire! Pass a poor body's door with never so much as a look or a 'good night'!"

Mr. Threlby turned and stared at Belle Catteral, as though he had not in the least taken in what she had said.

Belle dropped an obsequious curtsy, as she cried out:

"For the love of God, Squire, can't you spare a thought or a piece of silver for a poor widow woman, with never a one in all the wide world to say a kind word to her?"

"Why, I beg your pardon," he said with an absent-minded indifference.

Belle gave a laugh, which she accompanied with a bitter and an evil smile.

"No use begging folk's pardons when it's a bit of real hard cash they want to keep body and soul together!"

"Hard cash?" Mr. Threlby fumbled in his pocket. He had but one gold piece and a three-penny bit. "Why, here then!" and he handed her the silver coin.

Belle took it, looked at it scornfully, and then cried out in a fierce passion:

"Threepence! Threepence from the Squire of Boardale and Morley! Ha, ha! If he can only dress his own niece in rags, what can poor Belle expect?"

"You want locking up, my good woman!" he answered, not angrily, but with a tired indifference. "You keep too many whisky-bottles in your cupboard;" and he passed on his way.

He took no notice of the woman's squeal of rage, and forgot the incident as soon as it was over. He was so busy worrying over his own troubles that he took no notice even of the beautiful evening and the light on the fell, and before he knew it he was walking up his drive.

"Katherine at work!" he thought, as on entering the stable-yard he saw the lampshine behind her blind. "I must say for the girl that she works hard. But I thought that examination was over."

Then he stopped short. There was an unusual sound in the yard which made his heart beat quickly. It was the fascinating sound of a horse's hoofs. Yes, there was a horse standing haltered in his own stable-yard.

He went forward just as Roddy emerged from the dark stable, carrying the saddle and bridle.

Roddy, looking up, saw the tall, bowed figure and the clear deep eyes staring at him from underneath the heavy brows.

"And to what am I indebted for the pleasure——" began Mr. Threlby in his stiffest voice.

But though Roddy was shy of hearing poor Nell shriek, he was not shy of a stranger, and he guessed that this man must be Mr. Threlby.

"We have had an accident," he said. "My

father, Dr. Webster, and the district nurse are up there," and he nodded towards the window. Then, coming into the open, he flung the saddle adroitly across Nimrod's back.

His action drew the Squire's attention to the horse.

"Why, he has been down!" he exclaimed.

"Badly," said Roddy ruefully. "It happened coming over the fell. She would trot, and he stumbled, and she put out her shoulder, and——"

"But who?" demanded Mr. Threlby, thinking for an absurd moment that something had happened to Kitty.

"Nell—Nell M'Leod of the Quarries, you know. And your daughter invited us to carry her here, and I went for my father, and—well, they are at it now."

So Kitty was supposed to be his daughter! Mr. Threlby smiled curiously.

His first idea had been of extreme annoyance that anyone should dare to invade his privacy, but an accident was an accident, and a shudder passed through his frame.

Once before there had been an accident, and his own beautiful Molly had been carried up to that very house. He remembered how he had ordered off his man to go and shoot the horse, as he lay with a broken back a mile away.

"You don't mean that the young lady is in danger?"

"Oh no!" said Roddy; "it's only her shoulder. It can't be fatal, but it will be very beastly. I am just going to take her horse to the vet. He ought to have gone ages ago, but nobody has had any time." Then, realizing that of course Mr. Threlby would know all there was to know about horses, Roddy added eagerly:

"Please, would you mind looking at him? Do you think he is done for? Nell will break her heart if he is."

Mr. Threlby dropped his heavy bag, and, going up to Nimrod, he knelt on one knee and began undoing a bandage, while Roddy waited in a quiver of excitement.

"Who tied him up?" he asked.

"I think it was Kitty—your daughter," said Roddy.

"Well, go into the porch and fetch me out that lantern," he ordered briskly.

Roddy found the lantern, lighted it, and then held it down towards the wounded knees.

"Steady, old man!" said Mr. Threlby in a soft, reassuring voice, and Nimrod seemed to understand, for he put his nose down and touched Mr. Threlby's bent back affectionately.

"Do tell me, please," said Roddy anxiously.

"The right is a mere scratch, and the left—it is quite a clean cut—an inch at least; but it hasn't got to the bone, otherwise he would have been ruined."

"And now?"

"The damage will always show a little—it is a great pity—but he will get over it."

"Do you think I might ride him to the vet's, or ought I to lead him?"

" He had better stay here over Sunday. I will see to him myself," said Mr. Threlby decidedly, and there was a new cheerfulness in his voice.

Horse-love had come over the Squire in a rush. He couldn't possibly let the wounded beast out of his sight. He had not touched a horse since his wife had been killed.

Yet even as he gave Nimrod the invitation, he thought of the bedding and the food.

" Just run down the drive and round to the right, to Birkett's. You know the cottage?"

Roddy nodded.

" Ask him to oblige me with some bedding and hay."

" I'll bring it myself," said Roddy readily.

" If you don't mind."

" I don't mind anything except seeing poor Nell and hearing her scream. Listen to that!"

A low moaning could be heard distinctly.

Mr. Threlby looked up silently towards the open window. He understood the boy's feelings only too well.

" I know she is only coming out of the chloroform, and yet I can't stand it. I always was a fool that way."

" We are most of us fools in one way or another," said the man, as though to himself.

" I suppose," said Roddy, as a sudden idea came to him, " that you are the real Mr. Threlby?"

" I am Mr. Threlby, at your service!" Roddy's bright, comical expression forced a smile to the Squire's lips.

"I wonder whether it is a kind of good luck that we have all come bursting in upon you like this?"

"I am sorry I don't understand you."

"Only, I mean, about the Scheme."

"The Scheme! What Scheme?"

"Morley Model Village, Limited! We are stuck, you know, because you would rather not sell your land. But it really is the only possible site for the cottages—out of the blast of the wind, you know—and Tim and Nell and I were quite sure that if you only understood——"

"Suppose you run off, my lad, to Birkett's!" interrupted Mr. Threlby snubbingly. "The sooner we get this beast settled the better. I'll give him a good dose of hot ale. He has had a bad shake and a fright."

Roddy, knowing that his tongue had run away with him, darted off at double-quick time with rather a red face.

CHAPTER XIII

Twenty-four Candles

Now as soon as Marjory had done all she could for the nurse, she began worrying about hospitality, and she called Kitty into consultation.

" We ought to give the gentlemen some refreshment, Miss Kitty," she said anxiously. " And yet it doesn't seem fit to give them a meal in the Master's study—all in a muddle, and with him away too."

" Why not the hall?"

" That was what I was thinking," said Marjory doubtfully, "only——"

" Of course that is the proper place," said Kitty. " If you will see to the supper I will skirmish round and lay the table."

A great idea came to Kitty. Her uncle was safely away, so why should she not pretend for once that everything in the old house was as it really ought to be, and as Belle had told her it used to be long ago, when her beautiful Aunt Molly reigned there like a queen, and before her uncle took to his stupid miserly ways?

Belle was, indeed, the only one who had told her things about the old days at Threlby End, for when Kitty fished round to try to get news out of Marjory, the housekeeper snubbed her with a curious dignity.

"We won't talk about your uncle, Miss Kitty," she would say; "he mightn't like it."

But Kitty was now possessed with a wild idea that for once she would have her own way.

It was she who had invited the guests, and it was she who was responsible to do them honour. So she seized a duster and passed through to the front of the house.

Marjory kept the place as tidy as she could, but Kitty now fled round, dusting the oak sideboard, the mantelpiece, the old chairs, and the armour which hung on the walls, as far as she could reach.

Twelve brass sconces hung against the dark wainscoting, which supported two candles each, and Kitty made up her mind recklessly to do what she had often longed to do. The candles had gone yellow with age and were ringed with dust. She would light every single one!

But first she drew a shining oak table into the centre of the hall, and helped Marjory to set out some rare glass and plate, which she produced from a certain locked cupboard.

How Kitty loved beautiful things, and she went into raptures of joy as Marjory brought out the treasures!

"We must hurry, Miss Kitty," said Marjory. "I have put on a few potatoes, and it is lucky I had a chicken roasted for Sunday, and there's plenty of ham and fresh fruit, and I'll soon whip up some cream."

"That sounds all right!" said Kitty joyously.
"You leave me to put the finishing touches!"

But the moment she was alone she struck match
after match, and lighted every candle in the hall.

Then she stood back on the hearth-rug and stared
round her.

"It looks like a ghost house with all the ghosts
gone!" she said to herself. She was not quite sure
whether she wasn't feeling a little scared. Indeed,
her flesh went quite goosey when the door slid open.

"Oh, Don!" she gasped in relief, as the dog
pushed himself in and stood looking at her.

"I wonder—shall I blow them all out again?"

Then she gave a little laugh at herself. "No!
They would make a horrid smell. Courage! I'll
stick to what I have done."

She unbarred a wide French window, and passed
out on to the terrace, where she gathered a large
bunch of dew-dripping roses, and, returning, she
arranged them in an exquisite china bowl and
placed them carefully in the centre of the table.

"That was worth the trouble," she remarked to
Don. "The roses make the place feel more real.
Oh dear," and she sighed heavily, "I do wish this
all were real, and not a kind of a dream that comes
and goes! Goodness! I hear some of them coming!"

She stood back from the table, and caught sight
of herself in the long mirror, in her old black skirt
and her grubby white cotton blouse. If only she
could have managed to change into something
beautiful to match the room!

Then the door really did open, and she prepared

her politest smile for either the Doctor or Mr.
M'Leod.

"Uncle Jonathan!" she exclaimed in frank dis-
may. "You have come back?"

Mr. Threlby stood still in amazement at sight of
the flaring lights and the handsomely furnished
table, but perhaps most of all at the flushed excited-
looking girl in her shabby clothes.

He had for nearly a year looked upon Kitty as a
child, but there had been something in her manner
lately which had made him suspect that some day
or other she would grow up.

But now it galled him to notice that there was no
welcome in her tone. He was nothing but an un-
pleasant surprise to her.

"Yes, I am here," he said dryly. "And—who
has lighted the candles?"

"I did, Uncle Jonathan." Kitty flushed still
deeper.

"And why?" He asked the question in a certain
tone of intense politeness which Kitty could never
endure.

"I don't see why we should alway live as if—as
if we were in disgrace!"

The girl's hot words struck her uncle speechless

He stared round the hall, carried right away from
the present, back to the days of long ago.

Kitty's Aunt Molly had always insisted upon
having the candles lighted every night. She used
laughingly to tell him that the dark corners in the
old place gave her the creeps.

"Where is Marjory?" he demanded abruptly.

"She is getting the supper ready for the Doctor and Mr. M'Leod and the boys.   There has been an accident."

"Yes, I know."

"I had to ask the girl here.   I could not let her lie out on the fell for ever and ever!"

"No, that would have been a scandal," he said dryly.

"And then—I thought we ought to give them something to eat—decently!"

Kitty let her voice linger on the last word.   She was surely old enough to know how she was hurting her uncle.

"You are quite right," he said with a mild dignity which made her ashamed of herself.   "I will speak to Marjory."

Marjory met her master with some trepidation, and began to excuse herself the instant he entered the kitchen.

"Why should you apologize?" he asked.   "Make the best of us that you can."

They were interrupted by the apparition of a boy with dishevelled hair and bare legs, who, on seeing Mr. Threlby, paused uncertainly.

"You are back, then?" asked Mr. Threlby.

"It took a jolly lot longer than Father expected. But it was a beautiful job!" said Tim enthusiastically.   "Poor old Nell howled like winky-oh! But she couldn't feel anything really."

"My dear fellow, I meant did you get the hay and the straw?" and Mr. Threlby stared at Tim in a puzzled kind of way.

"Oh!" Tim's eyes twinkled. He was so accustomed to being mixed up with Roddy that he guessed what was wrong. "You think I am my brother, perhaps? But I am not—I am the other one!"

"They are Dr. Webster's boys, sir," explained Marjory. "They were riding with Miss M'Leod when the accident happened."

"And then I sneaked up into the room," said Tim eagerly, "and I saw Father truss poor old Nell up like a spring chicken!"

"I did not understand," said Mr. Threlby politely. "Then I will go out to the stable and see if your brother has returned."

CHAPTER XIV

After Supper

THE supper was quite a success. Marjory knew well enough how to do things, and she waited with smart dignity.

As for Kitty, she had felt herself so grubby in her everyday frock that she had crept noiselessly into her room and asked Nurse's leave to take her muslin frock from the drawer.

Kitty had never before seen her uncle in company with other men, and she was quite astonished to find how like other people he could be.

Evidently he knew Dr. Webster, and when Mr. M'Leod anxiously apologized for having given his household so much trouble, Mr. Threlby insisted that he was only delighted that his house had been so conveniently near.

Kitty was likewise impressed at the way in which her uncle behaved to her. He made her sit at the head of the table that she might pour out Marjory's delicious coffee, and he helped her first to a wing of the chicken, because she was the only lady present, and spoke of her ceremoniously as "my niece". Kitty began to wonder what had happened to the snubbed schoolgirl.

Now the boys were greatly excited at having actually delved into the very centre of this mysterious house; but in company with their father they knew it was as much as their lives were worth to be anything but their most proper selves. So they sat in silence, enjoying their supper and listening to the men's talk.

Yet all the time they kept expecting that Mr. M'Leod would begin about the Scheme. Now that he was actually face to face with Mr. Threlby it was a splendid chance to go hammer-and-tongs at the business.

Yet they talked of Nell, of horses, of motors, of all kinds of interesting subjects, upon which the boys themselves could have talked by the hour, but there was never a single word on the subject that really mattered.

Roddy got so far as to poke his father with his foot under the table and say "Scheme" with his lips, but Dr. Webster pretended that he did not understand in the least what he meant.

However, it was jolly to see the "champion" girl at such close quarters, and though it was rather disappointing that she had become so bashfully proper, she shone in the lingering glory of that high jump. Also, had she not helped to carry Nell down the fell, and done up Nimrod's knee like a professional?

"Well, Mr. Threlby," said Dr. Webster at last, "I will just run up once more to see how my patient is doing, and then I must leave her in your kind hands. Nurse is absolutely reliable, and to-morrow I hope she will have recovered sufficiently for me to send the ambulance van for her."

"Indeed, I simply do not know how to thank you," said Mr. M'Leod gratefully.

"It was my niece who thought of offering her bed, and I have been only too pleased to support her," he answered ceremoniously. "I only trust your daughter will make a complete recovery."

Tim rode Hop home, but when Roddy was safely tucked in beside Mr. M'Leod in the Doctor's car, he burst out:

"Oh, Mr. M'Leod, you never said a single word about the Scheme!"

"You thought I would?" he answered dryly.

"Why not, when you had got him there so beautifully?"

"My dear boy, one gentleman doesn't immediately try to take advantage of another, who has just laid him under an obligation!"

"But it would have been so easy. He was in a jolly temper, and you could have struck while the iron was hot!"

"It couldn't have been done, Roddy," laughed Mr. M'Leod. "You are a very wise person, no doubt, but not quite wise enough yet!"

CHAPTER XV

The Talk after Supper

"GOOD NIGHT, Uncle Jonathan," said Kitty rather shyly.

Marjory had cleared all the plate and glass from the table, and only the flowers remained. The candles were burning low, and Mr. Threlby had flung himself into a great arm-chair. He sat upright, startled by his niece's soft voice, and said nervously:

"Good night. That is—are you very tired?"

"Oh no!" she answered in surprise.

"Then, my dear, will you come here?"

"Yes, Uncle Jonathan."

She came and stood at attention on the other side of the fire-place.

"There is something I wish to say to you," he began. "Will you be good enough to sit down?"

Kitty sat down and waited. She was wide enough awake with the excitements of the last few hours, and she had been thankful for all the fuss which had driven her moping thoughts to the "back of beyond".

She noticed that her uncle was finding it difficult to begin, and her curiosity grew. What did he want to say? Was he going to give her a lecture about something?

"I think that you are somewhere about fifteen, are you not?" he asked.

Kitty went burning red. "I was fifteen to-day." She gave the defiant shake of her head which her uncle had learnt to know.

"It was your birthday to-day!" he exclaimed.

"Yes."

"I did not know. You—you must pardon me, Katherine."

"Oh, it didn't matter!" said Kitty. "Nobody knew, of course. Besides, I have had my birthday party to-night!" and she gave an uncomfortable laugh.

There was a long pause after that, and Kitty wondered if this was all her uncle had to say to her.

"I am very sorry that I have not realized your birthday," he said at last. "And this is hardly the day on which I like to tell you what you ought to know."

Kitty looked at him with big eyes and said nothing.

"I am afraid that I may hurt you. Yet I believe that you would rather——"

"Oh yes, please!" she interrupted breathlessly. She was feeling ashamed of her petulance, for her uncle's face looked strained and anxious. What could he have to tell her? What other strangeness was this day to bring forth?

"You have, I think, always thought that your father was killed in the South African War?"

Kitty was all mad attention now.

"But—I regret to say—I mean—this was not so!"

"You regret that my father wasn't killed?" she cried incredulously.

"No, no!" he said, thrown into confusion by her manner. "I mean that it was a pity that there was a mistake in the paper—a wrong number——"

"Then my father is alive! You mean that?" she cried, clasping her hands together. She did not know how her dark eyes were burning.

"No, no, not quite that!" her uncle struggled on. "Your father was alive—but he died later."

"When?"

"It was about two months ago—that is, in April of this year."

Mr. Threlby stooped to knock out the ashes of his pipe against the hearthstone. Not that he had any idea of smoking, but he wished to give Kitty time to take in the meaning of what he had said.

"You tell me that my father was alive last April?" Kitty spoke slowly, as though she were pleading with her uncle to take back his words.

"Yes, my dear," he said pitifully.

"But my mother did not know that my father was alive?"

"I am afraid not."

Kitty sprang up.

"It isn't true! You are making it up, Uncle Jonathan!" she stormed.

"I only wish I were, Katherine."

"But how do you know?" The girl was all on fire.

"I have just been up to London to see your father's lawyer. There can be no doubt that your father has been living in South Africa for some years. He died this spring of typhoid fever. His will and other papers have been brought over to England by a friend."

"His will?" faltered Kitty. She was trying hard to battle with the storm of thoughts that rushed through her brain.

"He fortunately made a will."

"But why fortunately? He was quite poor! He must have been quite poor—worth nothing!"

"Why do you think that?"

To tell the truth, Mr. Threlby was afraid of the passionate girl. He did not understand in the least how to deal with her.

But at his question Kitty gave a queer, half-hysterical laugh.

"Because if he had been rich, if he had had even enough to pay his passage, he would have come back to Mother and me!"

Mr. Threlby simply dared not answer her. How could he tell her the real truth? How could he tell her that his careless, selfish brother had deserted his wife and child so that he might enjoy himself as he chose out in the wilds of the Transvaal? Had he not told her enough for one night?

But Kitty was not going to let him off one word.

"Uncle Jonathan, was my father rich when he died?"

"He seems to have made a good deal of money in gold-mining and diamond shares. Before he

died he made a will, leaving it all to your mother
and——"

"But it is too late.   My mother is dead!"

Kitty's self-control broke down.   She sank back
in the big chair, and, leaning her head down, she
sobbed in great heaving gulps.

Her uncle sat tongue-tied.   How could he comfort the child?   He could not think of a single
excuse for Kitty's father.   Indeed, Robert Threlby
had behaved as a father just as he had behaved
as a boy—selfishly and meanly; and as all selfish-
ness ends in cruelty, so he had behaved cruelly
indeed to the wife and daughter he had deserted.

As for the fact that Robert had made a fortune
for himself, while he owed his brother tens of thousands, Mr. Threlby scarcely thought of that at all
just now.

Why could he not jump up and put his arms
about his niece and try to comfort her?

Alas, he knew that he had never given her any
real welcome into his home, and had never once
tried to win her love and confidence!   It was too
late to expect that she would turn to him now that
she was in such trouble.

Kitty gulped on, and at last her uncle's silent
presence seemed to exasperate her.

She flung herself out of the chair, swaying as she
did so, and was about to dart from the hall, when
he sprang up and put an arm about her.

"Katherine, my dear child!"

"Oh, please don't, Uncle Jonathan!" she cried,
pushing him off.   Then she escaped to her room.

It was but a tiny bedroom that Marjory had prepared for her. Everything felt suddenly strange and awful, and, setting her candle down, she flung herself on her knees by the bed and sobbed in a dreadful home-sick kind of way.

"Oh, little mother," she sobbed, "and we might have been happy all the time! And if we had had the money you could have gone sooner to the doctor, and perhaps you needn't have died!"

Flooding memories came over her of how her mother had toiled and contrived in her poverty, and how they had always spoken with such pride of the husband and father.

"Your father was a noble gentleman, Kitty, always remember that!" her mother would say.

Yet, behold, it was all a horrible mistake!

Kitty had brought from London the very portrait of her father which had always stood on her mother's dressing-table.

Why, Marjory, thinking to give her pleasure, had brought it from the sick-room and set it on the old chest of drawers!

Kitty sprang up impulsively. She seized the photograph and dashed it to the floor, shattering the glass to fragments.

Then she knelt down again and cried repentantly, as a horror came over her of what she had done.

"I don't care!" she insisted passionately. "He deserves it!"

Yet she picked up the picture of the khaki-uniformed soldier and examined it again. It was a handsome face, with fine eyes and a weak mouth.

"And you deserted mother — the best woman who ever lived! Mother, would you say that one ought to forgive even that?"

Kitty would like to have torn the photograph across and across in her rage. Yet somehow she laid it on the chest of drawers face downwards.

There was an odd sound against the door.

Kitty opened it, and Don came waggling in.

"Oh, Don!" she groaned. "You are the only friend I have in all the world!"

Miserable and forlorn, Kitty crept into bed, and Don jumped up and cuddled himself down at her feet.

CHAPTER XVI

The Boys Get Up Early

NELL had passed a wretched night, and indeed she declared to Nurse that she had not slept a single wink.

This was one of Nell's exaggerations, for she was not used to lying awake and took to it badly; but she cheered up amazingly when Kitty appeared with a dainty tray of breakfast, gay with a vase of pansies.

"I don't see how I am to eat a thing when I am stuck down like this," she giggled.

"Do let me help her, Nurse, while you go down for your breakfast," urged Kitty.

"Very well," said Nurse pleasantly. "I think you won your preliminary nursing diploma yesterday, so I ought to be able to trust you."

So Nurse departed, and Kitty, thankful to have something real to do, managed to feed Nell, not perhaps according to first-class hospital style, but well enough.

"You do it awfully nicely," said Nell patronizingly. Then she broke into a foolish chuckle.

"What is the joke?" asked Kitty.

"Only it is so frightfully funny to think that

Roddy's champion is sticking bits of toast and butter and marmalade into me. You couldn't have guessed such a thing would have happened, if you had guessed for a hundred years."

Kitty laughed merrily.

"I might as well begin my hospital training at once."

"Are you going to be a hospital nurse?"

"I told Tim that if he set up for being a fashionable doctor I would be his nurse in uniform to give him style!"

"I wouldn't be a nurse!" said Nell. "You might have to wheel a Bath chair. I should hate wheeling Bath chairs. I saw heaps of them once at Buxton when Daddy thought he was starting in rheumatism—it was really too much sugar in his coffee and marmalade. Besides, you can't go and do things for Tim. It was Roddy who bagged you. You are his champion."

"It was very kind of him," laughed Kitty.

"Oh, but it isn't a joke!" said Nell, turning solemn. "You'll have to be jolly careful or there will be a rumpus. You see, Tim rather gets things that belong to Roddy. He chose quite another girl. She had a snub nose and a freckled face, and you haven't a single freckle. You've that lovely soft tawny kind of a skin. I adore it!"

Kitty's face beamed. It really was a relief to have something to joke about.

"Kitty! Do you think they will want to wheel me in a Bath chair? I should shriek if Daddy had to turn into a chairman!"

" Perhaps you have a car?"

" Oh, well, we have—but you can't potter in the village in a car!" Then Nell's voice changed as she said wistfully: " Do you know, when I was quite a kid, I had a mother. Whenever I'm seedy, I simply ache for her."

" Yes," Kitty nodded, and her cheek began to burn.

" When you are jolly and happy you forget. I used to think that I would never forget, but I do!" and she sighed. " Only, even when one forgets, one has her there always—down in the cockles of one's heart!"

Again Kitty nodded.

" I suppose you haven't a mother either?"

" No."

" Did she die just a little while ago?" asked Nell, looking at Kitty's black skirt. It was the one she had had for her mother's funeral, and she had worn it for " best" ever since. It had been let down until it could bear no more.

" About a year ago," said Kitty.

" Then you must have had a birthday since then. Aren't birthdays squirmy things when you haven't your mother?"

" How do you mean?" though Kitty knew quite well what Nell meant.

" Well, you sort of feel that your father is making believe to be jolly, and all the time he is feeling squirmy and struggling. Only——" Nell gave a little start and blushed violently. " Perhaps you haven't any father either?"

"No."

"You have only Mr. Threlby?" Nell spoke dubiously.

"Yes; I have only Uncle Jonathan. Why——" she ran to the window.

"It's the boys!" cried Nell joyously. "I know it is!"

It was indeed. Roddy and Tim were riding soberly into the yard, though their horses were hot.

"Hush!" said Roddy to Kitty, putting his finger to his lips.

"She is wide awake," said Kitty, as she leaned out of the window.

"Rather!" squealed Nell. "Come on up! No, tell them to go and look at Nimrod first."

The boys were off their horses in a moment, and, having tied them up, they went into the stable to examine Nimrod; but, as they dared not meddle with Mr. Threlby's lovely bandaging, they were really none the wiser.

Then they knocked at the kitchen door and Marjory opened it.

"Good morning!" they said in one breath.

"Good morning, Nurse!" said Tim professionally; "and how is my patient this morning?"

Nurse knew these boys intimately, and she rose with mock ceremony, as she answered:

"She has passed a fair night, sir, but the limb is causing a good deal of irritation."

"That was to be expected," said Tim, frowning wisely. "Pray, sit down, Nurse. Don't let me disturb you.   I will go upstairs and feel the patient's pulse."

"Now you just be careful!" exclaimed Nurse, changing to her more ordinary manner.   "Five minutes is all I can allow."

"That will be heaps!   We'll manage to rouse the patient into a raging fever in that time.   Come on, Roddy!"

"Feeling an awful wreck, Nell?" asked Roddy sympathizingly, after both boys had shaken Nell's left hand.

"Rather!   It aches abominably!   I just feel as if I had been thrashed all over."

"Considering that you have never had a thrashing in your life——" began Roddy.

"That is really what is the matter with her," continued Tim.

"I have heard certain persons describe their feelings," retorted Nell.   "But—I don't see how you two got here so early."

"Quite simple," said Roddy.   "Got up early."

"And the female parent is away for the weekend," added Tim.

"Oh!"   Nell quite understood.

"Have you had any breakfast?" Kitty put in her word.

"We have and we haven't," said Roddy.   "But we wouldn't dream of adding to our sins by bothering you about our inner men."

"And now, may I feel your pulse, madam?" said Tim.   He took out his gun-metal watch, and seated himself by the bed.

"Silly!" said Nell, but she let him have her wrist.

"Afraid she has had too many snick-snacks in the night, Nurse," he remarked reprovingly to Kitty. "I regret to have to say that these amateur efforts in nursing are the plague of the medical profession!"

"Don't take any notice of him," said Roddy to Kitty. "He's only playing the goat."

"I like that," said Tim. "Play the goat, when one's heart is burdened with excruciating agony!"

"How is Nimrod, Roddy?" asked Nell.

"Oh, he's all right!"

"You are as red as a radish! You have just told a horrible lie!"

"No, I haven't. He will be all right. I mean, Mr. Threlby is looking after him splendidly, and he told me he wouldn't be lame."

"But it will show?"

"It will be bound to show a bit; but the right knee is almost nothing—a mere scrape."

"Why don't you shake me to bits?" demanded Nell, with a groan.

"Because I should, as your medical adviser, decline to allow it," struck in Tim. "It might lead to complications."

"He really will be all right by the time you can ride him again," said Roddy earnestly.

"I'd like to have him up here and hug him!" said Nell. "The darling!"

"How he would adore it!" teased Tim.

"I say, Roddy,"—the boy came nearer—"tell

(G 781)   E him I'm awfully sorry," she whispered. "Beg his pardon for me."

"All right," Roddy whispered back.

"But, Nell, we've something frightfully exciting to tell you," said Tim. "That Suffragette did hold a meeting in Morley. There were lots of people there, and it was as good as a play. The people roared."

"They were rude, of course—she was a woman, all alone. I wish I had been there. I would have stood by her."

"She didn't need anybody to stand by her," laughed Tim. "She gave them quite as good as they gave her."

"There may be something in what she said," admitted Roddy; "but women are always in such a mad hurry—why can't they wait——?"

"Wait for a million million years—oh, yes!" cried Nell.

"Five minutes up," said Nurse, coming in.

"And I think it is quite time," said Kitty, her face all alight with fun. "Life is getting too exciting."

"Yes; and we ought to be cutting, or the psalms will go wrong in church," said Roddy.

"Why, it's Sunday!" exclaimed Nell. "I quite forgot."

"Do you sing in church?" asked Kitty.

"We both chirrup like archangels," said Roddy. "I say, you know, you'll have to come over to Morley and let us hear the fiddle. We rather fancy ourselves in the musical line."

"I'd like to come awfully," said Kitty.

"Depart!" said Nurse. "Clear yourselves away, please! Any news about the ambulance?"

"Address me, please, Nurse," said Tim. "I am the medical authority. Yes. I heard the patient's papa talking of sending the ambulance van this morning, with an escort of the quarry fife and drum brigade. They will be here about twelve o'clock."

"Tim!" remonstrated Nurse; "you will say anything."

"And they are getting a perfect tyrant of a hospital nurse from High Rigg. You are a shorn lamb beside her, Nurse."

"We heard it all through the telephone," said Roddy.

"Oh! what really happened?" cried Nell.

"I'll describe the circumstances," said Roddy grandly. "It was like this:—

"'Are you there?'

"'Blank—blank—blank.'

"'Is it the Matron?'

"'Blank—blank—blank.'

"'You are quite sure she is strong enough?'

"'Blank—blank—blank.'

"'Sorry; but if she only weighs thirteen stone she is no use.'

"'Blank—blank—blank.'

"'You don't understand. Patient very wild—a regular terror—insists on rooms full of visitors—brass bands in her bedroom—and dancing niggers every night.'

"'Blank—blank—blank.'

"'Nurse Samson, did you say? She sounds better.'

"'Blank—blank—blank.'

"'Weighs eighteen stone, and a fist of iron? Just the kind we want. Send her right along.'"

"Roderick Webster, will you kindly depart?" interrupted Nurse, as Nell went off into dangerous giggles.

"Come on, you idiot! Can't you see that you are exciting my patient?" said Tim.

"Love and kisses, Nell beloved!" said Roddy, as Nurse seized him by the shoulder.

"So long!" said Tim.

And at last they were got out of the room.

"Aren't they killing?" said Nell. Yet she sank back looking rather white.

"They don't cross this threshold again," said Nurse. "Is the pain very bad?"

"Pretty well," admitted Nell. "But they couldn't tell. I managed to take them in, didn't I? You see, I disgraced myself so dreadfully yesterday."

"We won't think anything more about yesterday," said Nurse cheerfully. "Now, let me see how much of you I can wash before the doctor comes."

CHAPTER XVII

Sunday Afternoon

THOUGH Roddy's nonsense was nonsense, there was a touch of truth in it.

When Dr. Webster arrived, accompanied by Nell's father, they decided that the best plan would be to get the girl home, and establish her with a hospital nurse. So about midday the ambulance van arrived.

Kitty hovered about all the morning, doing any little thing she could, and she completely won Nell's heart by her merry kindness.

Nell began to long to know more about this beautiful dark girl who lived alone in this mysterious house.

"Kiss me, Kitty," said Nell, as she was about to be lifted into the ambulance; "and promise faithfully that you will come and stay sometime."

"Perhaps in the holidays," said Kitty, knowing that her uncle was within earshot.

"I won't have any 'perhaps'," said Nell. "I shall be stuck for ages. I know what a fiend Dr. Webster can be when he likes. But the boys would be in and out too, and would give you a good time. And we would motor, and I would play your accompaniments with my left hand. You really wouldn't have half a bad time."

"Why, of course I shouldn't," said Kitty. It was jolly to be wanted, and it was certainly a long time since she had had any real fun.

"Good-bye, Mr. Threlby," said Nell, "and thanks awfully. You will let Kitty come, won't you? You see, you must confess that it is frightfully dull for her here."

"Yes, I must confess that," said the Squire. "She shall certainly come if she wishes it."

Nell was laid down in the ambulance, and when she was comfortably settled, her voice cried out:

"Oh, Mr. Threlby, are you keeping Nimrod?"

"For a day or two," he answered, looking in upon her.

"It is perfectly angelic of you!" she said. Then her lip quivered, and Mr. Threlby turned abruptly away.

So at last the van drove off, and Mr. Threlby and his niece were left alone.

Now Kitty was simply dreading this time, for it was no use pretending that things could ever be the same again, and her shyness was growing upon her.

The usual Sunday arrangement had been quite upset by what had happened.

Punctually at ten o'clock uncle and niece usually set off for a small dale church about half an hour's walk away, and this Sunday walk was one of the few occasions on which Kitty had a chance of getting to know her uncle.

Sunday Afternoon 135

Sometimes they were quite silent. Sometimes they made conversation about the trees, the flowers, and the habits of animals and birds. On such subjects Uncle Jonathan was a mine of information, and Kitty was keen to learn from him what she could.

Just as they reached the lich-gate, Mr. Threlby always put his finger and thumb into his breast pocket, and ceremoniously handed Kitty sixpence for the offertory.

Then, while she waited in the porch, her uncle went round the church to lay a few fresh flowers on his wife's grave.

Kitty had never seen her aunt's grave, and she had always felt too shy to ask her uncle if she might go with him.

To-day, as soon as lunch was over, and Kitty was wondering what would happen next, Mr. Threlby remarked:

"If you will be ready at half-past four, we will go to the evening service."

"Yes, Uncle Jonathan," and Kitty escaped.

Mr. Threlby was relieved to be alone, for he had a great deal to think about, and had not even opened the week's accumulation of letters which Marjory had put on his desk.

The fact was that he had not even yet managed to tell Kitty all the story.

The money left to her mother had come to her, and the will had installed Mr. Marmaduke, the London lawyer, as her legal guardian.

"Robert hadn't even enough confidence in me to

leave his daughter under my guardianship," he thought bitterly. "But perhaps he was right. Certainly I don't seem to be the right man to make a young girl happy."

Presently, as he stared vacantly out from his window, he noticed that Kitty and Don were setting out for a walk. The girl was running with the dog, and she jumped clean over a shrub, while Don, barking ecstatically, ran round it.

He smiled grimly.

"She won't care," he mused. "As soon as she really understands how rich she is she will be quite happy. She is like her father—she wants money. She thinks that money is the royal road to happiness—poor child!"

He rose, and during the quiet of the Sunday afternoon he set out to make a tour of inspection of the old home.

He did not shirk any part of the place, but went into room after room, and pulled back the blinds to let in the light.

He did not even miss the old Threlby nursery.

Once he had thought that children of his own would shout and play there. But, alas! none had come.

What was that standing in the corner, hidden away under a covering?

He lifted the sheet, and suddenly tears started to his eyes, and he wasn't ashamed of them. All he saw was a battered old grey rocking-horse.

He had ridden him, flogged him, petted him, pulled hairs out of his tail, plaited his mane, ornamented him with ribbons, and bandaged him for pretended accidents. When dragged off to be bathed and put to bed he had howled.

He gave a harsh laugh at himself.

"I'm just a sentimental old fool," he murmured.

He sat down in the old window-seat, and looked at the initials cut in the woodwork by wicked young mischief-makers, and began to think bitterly of the jokes an auctioneer might make if he sold that old battered horse.

For Mr. Threlby was slowly making up his mind to sell up his estate and go away. He had only to get Kitty happily settled somewhere, and then he could wander off anywhere—what did it really matter?

He replaced the dust-sheet and then turned away. He would have time just to examine his letters before Marjory brought him a cup of tea.

Very few letters came to Threlby End nowadays, but amongst a number of circulars he found two notes of interest.

One was from Mr. M'Leod, urging him with great politeness to reconsider his decision about selling the Fold Field.

"I feel sure that if you understood how desperately the cottages are needed you would do your best to help us," so the letter ran.

"Understand!" he tossed the letter down.

He supposed that all the county was talking about him as a grudging landlord, who cared nothing about the wants of the poor.

Poor Molly! If his wife had lived, they had intended to have Morley rebuilt! He had the plans laid away in a drawer in that very room. Why had he not done it? Why had he let his own private sorrow spoil him for doing good to his neighbours? He knew he had done wrong. Then why couldn't he turn right-about-face and do right?

"I will soon answer that letter," he thought bitterly. "I will have a poster put out announcing a sale by auction of all the valuable property of Threlby End, Morley, and Boar Fell. Then anyone can buy anything they want, and they can turn this place into an orphan asylum for anything I care."

Then he opened the second letter. It bore a Canadian postmark, and Mr. Threlby knew the handwriting well.

It was from an old schoolfellow named Jack Holt, who had been his fag at Eton.

Jack had gone out years ago to Saskatchewan, to try his luck at farming, and after a struggle he was doing well. His letters were always refreshingly full of life and "go", and Mr. Threlby's face brightened.

"DEAR OLD BOSS,

"Forty-nine! I suppose you must be that by this time, for I am forty-six. That last letter of yours gave me the hump. Sorry I have been such an age in answering. Whatever can you find to do in your ancestral wigwam when you have sold off all your horses? You'll go off

your head, my dear chap. Come out here by the
next boat, and help me to break horses. I'll give
the whole lot into your charge—and I have some
grand young beasts.

"You can drive a team, or help to pack peaches,
and sing songs to us at night. Turn up before the
winter, and we will show you that there is fun in
the wide world yet. Then what about the charming niece? She surely can't fancy the style of life
you describe, that is, if she is any good. She
might as well be chucked into a convent.

"Anyway, don't make the girl an excuse. Rake
up your thousands and bring them along with you,
and we will put you in the way of taking the next
farm to ours. It is glorious land! Makes your
hair curl to look at it.

"There is my wife calling! She wants me to
go and see her bath our youngest. I have seen
the process before, but go I must. I have five
of them now, and they keep us lively. They want
an uncle badly to smack 'em, for their Daddy daren't.
So take pity on us and cable that you will come,
so that we may start fattening the calf.

"Yours,

"THE YOUNG-UN."

Mr. Threlby laid down the letter and passed his
hand across his forehead. It was extraordinary
that such a letter should have come at that precise
moment.

It was no use pretending that his heart hadn't
given a sudden spring of hope. Break horses for

the Young-un? Why not get rid of his old life
and start again?

But there was Katherine. He frowned. Katherine would not care—she was an heiress. She
was quite independent of him, for the fortune
would bring her in at least a thousand a year—
quite enough for any young girl to squander. He
wondered whether Katherine understood that this
money would come to her?

He stuffed the letter into a drawer, and strolled
out to see Nimrod.

Yet at the stable door he paused. There
was someone in the loose-box talking to the
horse.

He peeped in. Katherine was standing with her
arm about Nimrod's neck, kissing his nose.

He stepped back. Of course! Kitty had once
burst forth that she too adored horses.

He slunk away, in case she should guess that
he had seen her.

Now punctually at half-past four Kitty knocked
at her uncle's door, feeling decidedly shy in view
of the coming walk.

But she looked at him with surprise. What had
happened?

Kitty could see that some change had come.
Her uncle's face seemed to have broadened, and
he spoke to Don in his cheeriest way; for Don
always expected to come to church, and settled
himself down to wait outside until the service was
over, with great patience.

As a rule, Kitty did not enjoy going to church.

The Vicar was old, and had no roof to his mouth, and the harmonium squeaked agonizingly. A shoemaker with a broad Westmorland accent led the responses and the hymns, and the congregation consisted almost entirely of a few children seated in front.

In London, Kitty used to go with her mother on Sunday evenings to a great service in Whitfields, where she listened to an orchestra for an hour, and afterwards to one of the most inspiring preachers in London.

But that world had faded away, and Kitty had had to learn her way through the Prayer Book as though she were in a strange land.

But to-day, as she looked towards the vestry door, she was surprised to see a visiting clergyman in the crushed white surplice.

Her attention was attracted, and as the little group of people stood up, the stranger looked round quietly, as though waiting for attention before he spoke the opening sentence.

"Repent ye, for the kingdom of heaven is at hand!" He said the words in a clear full voice. Then, after another penetrating pause, he went on with the service.

This man's voice was a joy to listen to, and Kitty actually found herself quite impatient for the sermon.

Usually she settled herself to endure it as best she might, and tried hard to think of something else. But now she wondered what this stranger would speak about on this hot Sunday. The

church felt close, and was scented with a queer
mixture of dankness, of the honeysuckle which
peeped in at the windows, and of the roses worn
by the children.

"Repent ye, for the kingdom of heaven is at
hand!"

That was the text of the sermon, and Kitty sat
forward.

"There are so few grown-up people here this
afternoon, that we will all be children together,"
the clergyman said quietly.

"Boys and girls." He looked first at the row
of children in front and then passed his eyes across
to the Squire's pew. Did he think that the tall,
dark-eyed girl of fifteen was a child too?

"I wonder what the kingdom of heaven is
really like? Of one thing I am quite sure. It is
a kingdom of love. Let me read you some of
the rules of the kingdom, and then let us honestly
try to find out whether we are keeping them. I
will read these rules from a new translation of a
very old book:

"'Drop all bitter feeling and passion and anger
and clamouring and insults, together with all
malice; be kind to each other, be tender-hearted,
be generous to each other, as God has been generous to you in Christ. Copy God, then, as His
beloved children, and lead lives of love, just as
Christ loved you and gave Himself up for you to
be a fragrant offering and a sacrifice to God.'"

There was something so real and keen in the
speaker's manner that the children listened in rapt

attention as he pleaded with them to enter into the kingdom of love.

"Why, children, one of the rules of the kingdom is that we must love those who have really wronged us and behaved badly to us. Listen to what the Master said one day—and you may be sure that the children were lying round on the grass at His feet:

"'Forgive, and ye shall be forgiven. Give, and it shall be given unto you, full measure, pressed, shaken down, and running over shall they pour into your laps, for with the same measure that you use, they shall measure to you in return.'

"Ah, boys and girls! when you are as old as I am you will know the pain and the trouble that come into families and into nations through the spirit of hate and unkindness.

"When you find that spirit creeping into your hearts, cry out to Almighty God to cast him out. He is a vile, unhappy spirit, and he will spoil all your lives if he can. Will you not rather be God's dear children of love?"

It was not a long sermon, and not one of the congregation thought of fidgeting.

When all was over, Kitty and her uncle left the church and walked some distance without speaking.

"I wonder," her uncle began at last, "whether you have realized or thought about what I mentioned to you yesterday — about the money, I mean?"

Kitty had been thinking about the sermon, and her conscience was pricking her uncomfortably, and at her uncle's question she answered perversely:

"I think it had all better go to the bottom of the sea!"

Her uncle laughed out.

"My dear child, that is foolishness. It will all come to you when you are of age; and meanwhile you will have a legal guardian, who will spend upon you what is right. This money will make a great difference to you, and I hope that you will be able to live somewhere where you will be really happy."

What was there in her uncle's cheerful words that gave Kitty such a pang of home-sickness? Surely the very thing she wanted was money and independence? Had she not often dreamed how splendid it would be if she could get right away from Threlby End and her uncle?

But Kitty had begun to see that perhaps she had made a mistake; indeed, she hardly knew what she thought. She only felt that Uncle Jonathan's words hurt her.

"I suppose that you are my legal guardian, Uncle Jonathan?"

Kitty did not know that she was striding along faster and faster.

"Oh no, I have nothing whatever to do with your plans now! The lawyer, Mr. Marmaduke, is your guardian."

"You mean that I shall not be living at Threlby End any more?" she demanded, startled at his tone.

"No—oh, no!"

Mr. Threlby looked at his niece curiously. He expected this news would excite her. Surely she would be glad to know that she was rich and independent, and that she could live wherever she chose!

But if he had made a mistake about Kitty's feelings, she had also made a mistake about his.

A feeling of unreasonable bitterness swept over her. It was as clear as clear that Uncle Jonathan was thankful to be rid of her, and thankful to have Threlby End to himself once more. Very well. If he didn't care, she wouldn't care.

Mr. Threlby kept pace with her, now and then knocking off a thistle-head with his stick.

They had left the wood, and were walking along by the yew hedge. Then they turned in at the drive gate.

Kitty looked up at the familar house and neglected garden. Now suddenly, when she felt herself turned out, she made the startling discovery that she loved the place very dearly. Life was too utterly silly!

Then a fearful thought struck her, and she said quickly, and, as her uncle thought, eagerly:

"When do I go?"

"Just as soon as you like and it can be arranged," he said steadily.

"Yes," thought Kitty, "he is sick and tired of me, and longs to be rid of me."

"And when I go, may I take Don?" Kitty was mad that she could not keep her lip from quivering as she put the question.

"Why, certainly!" he answered her. He felt dreadfully hurt.

This niece, who had lived with him for a year, didn't mind a rap about leaving him. All she cared about was a dog!

Now it happened that a little later Marjory tapped at her master's study door.

"You wish to speak to me?" he asked.

"Yes, sir, if you can spare a minute. I have had some bad news. My mother has been taken ill, and my sister wants me to come home for a week or so if I can be spared."

"I am very sorry," he said sympathetically.

"You see, sir, my mother is pretty bad, and if I could possibly get away by to-morrow evening——"

"We must make it possible for you," he said heartily. "Of course you must go."

"But how will you, sir, and Miss Katherine manage? I have been worrying all day, and haven't liked to speak."

"There need be no difficulty about Miss Katherine. Either she can board at school or I may be able to accept an invitation for her which she received to-day."

"It is very good of you, sir," said Marjory gratefully.

"Not at all," he said briskly. "It will be quite convenient for me to shut up the house. I have business in High Rigg, and I shall stay at the Club. I may have to go to London again also."

"You are sure, sir?"

Mr. Threlby smiled.

"You are an old worrier, Marjory! Just cover over the furniture, and I will take the valuables with me to High Rigg; and send Miss Katherine in to me that I may tell her."

When Kitty came in, Mr. Threlby looked at her keenly.

"Katherine, Marjory is in great trouble. She wants to get away to-morrow; so, as neither you nor I can live here without her, I shall arrange for you either to board at the school or to accept Mr. M'Leod's invitation. I shan't know certainly until to-morrow; but you may as well be putting a few things together. I wish Marjory to get off at the earliest possible moment."

"Yes, Uncle Jonathan," said Kitty.

She rushed off to her own room. She had a weird feeling that this strange life had come to an end, and that after to-morrow she would never see the old place again.

She was too excited to be able to decide whether she was really glad or sorry.

CHAPTER XVIII

A Question to be Settled

"Oh, Madam Dear, isn't it truly awful?" said Nell.

It was Monday afternoon, and Mrs. Webster had hurried home on hearing of Nell's accident, and was now seated by her bed-side.

Mrs. Webster knew that Nell's daily governess would be terrified of taking any responsibility, and that Mr. M'Leod would be thankful indeed that the doctor's wife should give an eye to his unfortunate daughter.

"It might have been more awful, you poor wicked child!" she said in answer to Nell's appeal. "But the Doctor thinks you are doing splendidly."

"I don't think that any doctor knows what 'splendidly' really feels like!" sighed Nell. "Oh, Madam darling, if you only knew how I ache! I simply feel as if I couldn't bear the bandages another minute—as if I must fling my arm out somewhere. Do you really think that I shall be stuck here for ages?"

"I hope it will not be so very long, dear, before we shall have you sitting outside."

"But I shall only be able to sit; and——"

A Question to be Settled

"Yes, let me have all the grievances at once."

"Well," and Nell's mouth twitched funnily, "I shall get so awfully fat. I know I shall. And the boys will jeer more than ever. They really have been horrid about my adipose tissues ever since they came across Roddy's champion. I can't help it if I can't run a mile without taking breath, can I?"

"We must be careful of your diet," laughed Mrs. Webster. "Nurse and I shall have to consult. No more chocolates!" and she eyed a suspicious-looking box that was lying on Nell's side table.

"Oh yes; that was from that darling Mr. Gregory! Wasn't he sweet? You know he said that he would roll on his bed in anguish, and tear his hair out, if anything happened to me because of Nimrod's new shoe. But of course it wasn't the shoe at all. It was just my—my pig-headed-ness, you know," and Nell sighed again.

"Well, at any rate, I have a piece of news to cheer you," said Mrs. Webster brightly.

"Why, what?"

"Roddy's champion, as you call her, will be arriving in a few minutes at The Warren. So I shall have to run away and meet her."

"My mysterious girl?" cried Nell excitedly.

"I don't know about being mysterious. But it seems that their housekeeper has had to leave unexpectedly, and, as Mr. Threlby has business to take him away, the house has been shut up. Kitty went to school as usual, but her box has been sent on here, and she will arrive by the five o'clock train."

"But how did you get her?" asked Nell.

"Mr. Threlby sent a message to ask us to take her."

"Fancy him asking us to do him a favour when he won't sell us so much as a pennyworth of his land!"

"Still, he does not seem to have grudged offering hospitality to a certain reckless young lady, nor doing his best to mend up her horse, according to a report I have heard."

Nell flushed and said quickly:

"But it was I who invited Kitty."

"I know, dear; and perhaps in a week or two, when we see how you get on, you can have her. At present she must stay with us."

"She is Roddy's champion," said Nell warningly. "Don't go and let Tim bag her, Madam Dear. He chose that freckly one, and he ought to stick to her."

"You think you know poor Tim!" laughed Mrs. Webster. "But I must hurry off to the train."

"Is she frightfully poor?"

"Oh, Nell! your besetting sin—curiosity."

"Only, Madam Dear, she must have worn her very best frock for the prize-giving; and, really, it wasn't fit for the rag-bag."

"I am not going to satisfy foolish curiosity, Nell. You think far too much about clothes."

"Then do get her a really ducky frock while she is here. There is the Flower Show coming on, and, well—she couldn't appear in that old make-shift. She is so beautiful, too! It would be a positive shame!"

"Good-bye!" Mrs. Webster was at the door.

Now Kitty's visit to The Warren had been arranged so hurriedly that the boys knew nothing about it, and the shock was terrific when they plunged into the dining-room, hot and dusty from their ride, to find Kitty peacefully sitting at tea with their mother.

"Have manners deserted us?" inquired Mrs. Webster, as Roddy and Tim grasped each other by the arm and stood transfixed.

They bounced forward and shook hands.

"Remember, Kitty," said Tim earnestly, "that I am the one and only friend you have in this awful family!"

"I like that!" exclaimed Roddy. "I chose her out from amongst a hundred and thirty girls as my champion!"

"Don't wrangle over my visitor the first moment you set eyes on her," said Mrs. Webster. "If you would both depart and tidy up your most awful selves, that would be more to the point."

Mrs. Webster spoke with a cheerful authority which could not be disregarded, for a wash was an inexorable preliminary to tea with their mother; but the instant they returned they made up for lost time by shooting out question after question.

They wanted to know everything—why Kitty had come, how long she was going to stay, and very much besides.

Mrs. Webster turned away to her writing-table while the boys finished their tea, and presently

Roddy asked Kitty how long her lessons usually took her.

"Just as long as I let them," she answered. "Only I ought to do some fiddle practice."

"Then," struck in Mrs. Webster, who was quite capable of writing notes and attending to what was going on around her at the same time, "lessons and practising before supper, please, and then you can enjoy yourselves afterwards. I thought, Kitty, that you would prefer to work in your own room."

"I'd love to," said Kitty readily.

So Kitty retired to her sweet bedroom over the porch, where she found a writing-table, and her box already unstrapped.

She looked westwards across a strip of garden to the high road. Beyond the road the railway line wound right and left, and, far beyond, the splendid fells rolled one behind another to the skyline.

These fells were rich in evening colour, and Kitty interested herself in picking out Boar Fell, which rose a long way towards her left, and behind which poor old Threlby End lay deserted.

This day had been filled with strange excitement. Life had changed completely and so utterly unexpectedly. It was quite impossible to settle to ordinary lessons.

Kitty was turning from the window, thinking that she would unpack, when she was startled by hearing a low whistle, and, looking out, she saw that Roddy was sitting astride of the porch staring in upon her.

"Busy—doing nothing?" he inquired serenely.

"Y—es!" said Kitty slowly! "Only—is it usual for gentlemen to visit their lady guests in that style?"

"They always did it this way in Shakespeare," said Roddy. "Besides, I have come on urgent business, which must be settled at once."

"Really?"

"You needn't look so jolly unconcerned," said the boy in an aggrieved tone. "Now, what I want to know is, whether you admit that you belong to me, or whether you really prefer the medical student? Think hard before you decide. It was I who bagged you at the start—and I am miles nearer your age than Tim, even though he has sprouted up like an ill weed. Besides, he chose the freckly girl at the sports. Tim says that he helped you down the fell with Nell, and that that cancels that; but I should just like to know where we both are."

"But—why can't I be jolly with you both?"

"Oh, it's not exactly a question of being jolly! It is that Tim wants to back out of his choice. He backed the freckly girl, and you licked her into fits, and I ought to have the credit of you. Understand?"

"Not exactly. Besides, the freckly girl beat me into fits. Think of the prizes she won!"

"Oh, that's nothing!" said Roddy. "What would be the good of an armful of prizes if you had a mad bull after you and a hedge in front?"

Kitty laughed out. "Well, settle it between you. I'm willing either way, of course."

"That's not much of a personal compliment," said Roddy. "I'll repeat that remark to Tim."

Roddy favoured Kitty with a masterly wink, then slid down the roof, to the peril of his knickers, and dropped on the gravel footpath.

A few minutes later, curious sounds might have been heard proceeding from the schoolroom—muffled voices, banging of furniture, and other still more ominous noises.

The servants, hearing it, laughed.

"Master Roddy and Tim at it again," said Jennie, the housemaid. No one interfered when the boys fought. Explosions cooled the atmosphere.

"The freckly girl has nothing whatever to do with it!" cried Tim furiously. "You hooked it on the fell, and I did everything with her, and she doesn't know you from Adam!"

"You being Adam!" said Roddy cuttingly. "However, you will be glad to hear that I asked her just now which of us——"

"How could you ask her, when Mother sent her up to her lessons?"

"There is such a thing as a porch!"

"Oh, you sneaked!" sneered Tim.

"You would have done just the same if you had thought of it," retorted Roddy. "I asked her which of us she would have, and she said she didn't care a straw, and that we could fight it out between us."

"Then come on!" cried Tim.

So Roddy came on, and they fought hard, though, it must be confessed, not very scientifically.

It was Tim who finally fell, bleeding at the nose.

Roddy helped to mop him up, and then turned his attention to a river of ink that was meandering across the table.   He just saved a waterfall on the carpet by his handkerchief.

However, the affair was now settled, and when Kitty came downstairs a little later, to practise in the drawing-room, Roddy followed her, and, opening the piano, struck A, so that she could tune her fiddle.

"Have you settled things?" she asked comically.

"Yes; it is all over.   You're mine!"

"But what is over?"

"We fought.   I messed up Tim's nose."

"Oh, you didn't!" cried Kitty horrified.   "I thought that brothers loved each other."

"They do—at odd times," said Roddy.

"And now I suppose you have quarrelled, and that it will be horrid?"

"Why should it be horrid?   You don't take us for schoolgirls, do you?"

"That was a nasty one," said Kitty.   "Do you know, I had forgotten that boys were so queer.   I haven't spoken to one, until Saturday, for quite a year!"

"It's surprising, then, that you are as nice as you are," said Roddy.

"Roddy!" came a stern voice.   "Come out this instant!   Kitty wants to practise."

"All right, Mother.   I was only striking A for her."

CHAPTER XIX

They Roam

" IT seems that Nurse Samson has decided that Nell isn't to have any visitors to-night," said Roddy at supper.

"Not even us?" asked Tim reproachfully.

"Not even you," said his mother.

"Then, if Nell is off, I vote we roam," said Roddy. "Unless you are too tired, Kitty."

"Considering that I usually walk six miles every day of my life——"

"Then may we, Mamma?" asked Tim. "We'd like to show her the sights of the village. Far better than stuffing in on a fine night like this."

"So long as you are in by nine prompt," said their mother. In truth, she was thankful to be rid of them, for she was always busy.

Now Kitty was finding it impossible to be doleful while in the boys' company, so, as the three set off to "roam", she let herself go, so that she might get what fun she could.

But the boys had a plot in their heads which they had taken mighty good care not to reveal to their mother; for she would have nipped it in the bud, and their mother's nippings were no joke.

Kitty had by a special providence come to Morley from Threlby End. She was actually the unwilling landlord's own niece. A niece was supposed to be able to get anything she chose out of an uncle. They had only to get Kitty converted to the Morley Village Scheme, Limited, and the thing was as good as done. The plan was deliciously simple; but, as they were not quite sure whether Kitty knew anything about the Scheme, they had decided to go about the matter cautiously.

To test her ideas they took her round to the very worst cottages they knew of, on the plea of showing her something picturesque.

"You would love to see some of the simple beauties of Morley, wouldn't you?" asked Roddy alluringly.

"Rather!" said Kitty innocently.

"Well, we call this Squash Row," said the boy as they stood opposite to four dismal cottages. "Isn't the whitewash sweet?"

"And the dinted roofs?" added Tim. "They are made like that so that the kids can play at waterfalls tumbling down on their beds."

"But why Squash Row?" asked Kitty.

"Oh," said Roddy airily, "because they average about six kids in a room! They are all out just now, getting a last breath of air before going into the Black Hole for the night, you know."

Kitty looked puzzled. "But—if that is true—you are worse than a London slum."

"Oh, much worse!" said Tim enthusiastically. "That is what Morley prides itself upon. They all adore being squashed. It is so warm on a summer night, for the windows are so small and only bits of them will open."

"Except when Father smashes his stick through them," said Roddy.

"Then they rage and stuff them up with rags again," said Tim.

"The landlord ought to be ashamed of himself," said Kitty indignantly. "I hope he isn't anyone you happen to love?"

"We don't know him well enough," said Roddy regretfully. "But would it bore you to hear about the Scheme?"

"Not if it has anything to do with pulling down these horrible places," said Kitty keenly.

"Then fire ahead, Roddy," said Tim, with a wink at his brother.

So they strolled along the high road in the direction of the quarry, passing the Pump House on their way, while Roddy talked nineteen to the dozen as he described the whole Scheme.

Suddenly he stopped and cried out dramatically, as he waved his hand towards a large piece of land to the right of the road:

"And that is Fold Field. That is the one and only place where we can properly carry out what we want."

Kitty looked towards a broad stretch of rough land, backgrounded picturesquely by massive rocks and dotted about with low-growing trees.

As Roddy talked, it was clear that she was innocent of any knowledge of the Scheme, and it rejoiced the boys' wicked souls to find that every moment they were making her keener and keener.

"We want to build the houses in a semicircle, so that every house can have a sweet view and afternoon sun. We shall have a bowling-green and a playground for the kids, and everyone will have a piece of garden, and we want to keep as many of the trees as we can. See how sheltered it is!—the only sheltered place anywhere about— and, well, it will be ripping!" So Roddy finished up breathlessly.

"You mean, if we can get the site," said Tim.

"Yes—if!"

"But who is the landlord?" asked Kitty. "It is quite disgraceful that he should stand in the way of such a splendid idea."

But now that the critical moment had come both boys began to funk.

"Oh, well—perhaps we had better not say!" said Roddy. But he looked so odd that Kitty stared at him.

"A mystery?" she laughed. "Or perhaps this is all a cock-and-bull story, like the conversation on the telephone?"

Now a boy of fourteen does not like to be scorned by a girl of fifteen—especially a visitor who can jump like a boy and play the fiddle like a man. So Roddy, sighing deeply, said to Tim:

"Shall we tell her on condition that she promises to help?"

"But how can I help?" asked Kitty.

" Well, you see, you are his niece," said Roddy very nervously.

" What?" exclaimed Kitty incredulously.

There was something so tragic in the way the girl spoke that the boys were scared, and began to imagine what their mother would say if she knew what they had been up to.

" I'm awfully sorry—but it is true—it really is," said Roddy earnestly. " Only, I don't suppose Mr. Threlby has an idea how bad the cottages really are. That horrible lawyer, Mr. Taggart, at High Rigg, deceives him. And he can't really guess how tremendously we want the Scheme to go through. Mother says we ought to think the best, even of Mr. Threlby. But now that you have seen everything, you will be able to explain to him, won't you?"

But Kitty was absolutely dumb, and her teeth gripped her under lip.

" We thought," blundered Roddy, "that it would be such a lark if we could do something ourselves —just us three! Mr. M'Leod will tear his hair with mortification if we succeed where he has failed. He always scorns us and says we put our fingers in every village pie. But if we could cook this pie ourselves—we three, or perhaps Nell too—it would be such a crow!" So Roddy gabbled on, hardly daring to look at the visitor.

The fact was that Kitty didn't know what to think. She had often thought all kinds of evil against her uncle, but never such evil as this. Was he really such a miser that he could be quite happy to let a whole village live in bad conditions?

"Will you try what you can do?" pleaded Roddy. "Let's have a kind of *entente* between us four, so that we can support each other against the common foe."

"Don't be an ass," struck in Tim. "She can't be expected to touch this business if we call her uncle a foe."

"No," admitted Roddy. "Well, let's call him a dupe. Someone must have been getting at him, for he is really quite all right."

"How?" asked Kitty sharply.

"Well, it is no use pretending that——"

"Oh, do shut up, Rod!" said Tim. "You are making it worse and worse."

"I'm not going to shut up," he said. "It is no use for us to pretend that we haven't thought of Mr. Threlby as a kind of an ancient baron, gloating over people's misery. But now, since we have met him, we can't think that any more. He was so decent to Nell, and then there was Nimrod——"

"Yes; that's it," said Tim anxiously, feeling that somehow the whole plot had miscarried. "And you are his own niece, you know, and if you can get at him without any lawyers fussing, there's no knowing what you might do. He'll be certain to say 'yes' to you. Why, we could see that he treats you like a princess!"

"And then you will have done something grand for the Empire," urged Roddy. "Father says that every healthy child who grows up to be a good man or a good woman is a strength to the Empire."

But now the boys had really said all they had to say, and could but wait for the answer.

They turned and walked slowly back to the village, and at last Kitty said abruptly:

"I can't do what you want. Isn't it nearly nine o'clock?"

The boys looked at each other.

"Floored!" said Tim with his lips to Roddy.

"Yes, it's getting a bit late," admitted Roddy.

"Let's race back," said Kitty unexpectedly.

"Right oh!" they cried with relief. Kitty was not an offendy kind of girl after all.

So they raced to the smithy, and Kitty won easily.

"T' lass has it," remarked Gregory, as he sat on the seat outside his cottage door, smoking his pipe.

"Don't rub it in," panted Roddy. "What's the time?"

"Twelve minutes to nine."

"Ten minutes here and two minutes to get home," said Roddy.

"Oh, boys!" exclaimed the smith's daughter.

Florrie Gregory was a sweet-faced girl, wearing a smart pink overall, and she was busily crocheting as she stepped through the door.

"Oh, Florrie!" answered Tim.

"Do tell us about the accident. How is Miss Nell to-night?"

"Frightfully bad!" said Tim tragically. "They won't even let us see her."

"And if it hadn't been for the Good Samaritan of Threlby End—allow me to introduce her to you," said Roddy. "Miss Katherine Threlby, champion leaper, runner, fiddle-player, actress, and piles of other things!"

"Roddy!" expostulated Kitty.

"Glad to make your acquaintance, miss," said the smith. "And glad you were able to do summut for t' poor lass. I've worried fearful; but Nimrod's shoe was all right, that I'll swear, and I warned her to go easy."

"Nell knows it was her own fault," said Roddy. "Father says she won't be loose from her strappings for at least six weeks."

"And she was frightfully sick that she couldn't get to hear the beautiful Suffragette," said Tim.

"Yes; we hear you were quite bowled over, Florrie," said Roddy teasingly.

"I was nowt of t' sort!" cried Florrie indignantly. "A vote is right enough, and nobody can deny that a woman has as much sense as two men——"

"But not boys." Tim winked at Kitty.

"But that young woman—with all her blandishments—she'll not get me to want to upset the world for something that, goodness knows, when folk gets it, won't do them no good."

"You are just a stick-in-the-mud!" said Tim. "A miserable traitor to your sex!"

"And that daft Polly Dennison," Florrie went

on irately; "if I hadn't got hold of her, and if she hadn't been short of money, I do believe she would have set off to London then and there, to join in a big procession or summut! What good could a scatterbrain like her do? She'd best mind her own farm, and not drive her mother silly."

"We did some of Miss Dennison's work on Saturday," said Roddy. "Goodness! what is that wheezy old clock of yours saying, Florrie?"

"Don't you get insulting my clock," said the smith. "It belonged to my grandfather. It always does do a bit of sniffing two minutes before it strikes."

"Two minutes! So long!" cried Roddy. "Dash, all of you!"

But as they dashed they almost ran into a burly countryman who was tugging hard at a cord. And fastened to the end of the cord there was the most frantic thing in the dog line ever seen.

"Oh, Don!" shrieked Kitty.

The man let the cord go helplessly. Don was devouring his kneeling mistress.

"Why, behold the dog of dogs!" cried Roddy.

The dog was most certainly Kitty's, and the man was Samuel.

After wild questionings it turned out that he had taken Nimrod to the vet's, and had then, at Mr. Threlby's orders, brought the dog on to Morley.

This sign of her uncle's thoughtfulness gave Kitty a little stab, but she soon forgot it in the bliss of having her only friend in the world with her.

Don was now in danger of having his head turned by the warmth of his welcome, not only from his mistress, but from the boys.

"Where does he generally sleep?" asked Roddy, as he rubbed the dog industriously under the chin.

"On my bed," said Kitty.

"You'll never get the female parent to agree to that," said Roddy warningly; "she would have a fit."

But when they entered the house, Kitty dashed upstairs to take off her things, and Don followed her, perfectly at home wherever his mistress was.

"I hope you haven't tired Kitty out," said Mrs. Webster to the boys, as they dawdled about before wishing good night.

"Oh, I don't think so!" said Roddy. "She beat us in a race."

"Where did you take her?" asked their mother innocently.

"Just about," said Tim vaguely. But there was something in his way of speaking that set his mother on the alert.

"You have done something you shouldn't. What was it?"

Now Roddy and Tim had learnt by experience that it was better to be frank about their misdoings, and get "it" over, whatever "it" might be.

Roddy always found it easier to confess than Tim, and was usually the spokesman on awkward occasions; so now, with specious eloquence, he poured forth an account of the plot they had made, admitted its failure, and then waited for the descent of the avalanche.

It came.

"And how many times have I warned you against making mischief about things you hear in confidence in this house? Do you two boys intend that neither your father nor I shall ever talk over anything before you? You have done a right-down ungentlemanly piece of work. I wouldn't have had such a thing happen to a visitor of mine for anything. Go straight upstairs to bed, and neither of you are to say a word to the other until you appear at breakfast to-morrow."

The boys slunk away. The punishment was one they particularly detested.

But it would have to be endured, and the comfort was that when they met their mother at breakfast the storm would have passed as completely as though it had never been. That was the best of the "female parent".

CHAPTER XX
A Dog's Howl

"My dear, I do hope that you will be comfortable," said Mrs. Webster, as she escorted Kitty up to her room.

"Oh yes, thank you!" said Kitty shyly. It was strange that she should actually be staying with the charming little lady who had given away the prizes.

Don was supposed to be happy on some straw in the stable, and Kitty had not had the courage to ask that he might sleep with her.

Yet Kitty had fallen in love with Mrs. Webster's kind brown eyes. They were eyes to give confidence, even though they could sparkle with indignation at her own boys.

"If someone weren't indignant with them now and then I should like to know what would happen to the household?" Mrs. Webster had asked, and no one had ever been able to give her an answer.

It was strange what a way people had of coming to the doctor's wife in their troubles, and they always went away helped and comforted.

"She is better even than the doctor's medicine," more than one villager had been known to say.

And that was saying a great deal, for a "bottle from t' doctor" was supposed to charm away most things.

"Let me brush that great mop of hair for you, dear," said Mrs. Webster cheerfully.

"Oh no, please!" said the girl shyly.

Kitty didn't like to confess that she had not dared to pack her dreadfully shabby dressing-gown to come visiting.

"Nonsense! I should love to do it. Alas! I have no daughter, and Roddy and Tim's hair has long ceased to be any joy. It feels rather chilly. I don't suppose you have troubled to bring a dressing-gown. I will fetch one."

Kitty gave a little sigh as Mrs. Webster left the room. She must really make up her mind to meet any queer thing that happened.

"Here is a very old friend of mine," said Mrs. Webster as she returned. "Warm, but not elegant." Next minute she was brushing hard and skilfully, and talking about the school and the acting and other commonplace subjects.

Mrs. Webster could tell quite easily that, though Kitty responded politely and even brightly to her attempts at conversation, there was evidently something wrong.

"I won't press her to-night," she thought. "Yet a young girl living in that desolate house with such a curious man as Mr. Threlby can hardly have had a very gay time."

So, as at last she tied up the thick, shining plait, she said:

"You know that Nell wanted you to stay with her dreadfully, but I couldn't let you visit in such an invalid home. But you must go in as much as you like, and while you are here you must just put up with the boys."

"They are awfully jolly," said Kitty.

"They can be; but by their own account to-night I fancy they have been annoying and rude."

Kitty felt her face growing redder and redder, and, as she was seated before a long mirror, she could not hide the dreadful fact.

"It didn't matter," she blurted out.

"It is nice of you to say that. But I have told the boys that they are never to let such a thing happen again. I feel sure they worried you."

"It wasn't just that," said Kitty.

"There! Now you are finished; that has been a real pleasure," said Mrs. Webster, as she put down the brush and stood back.

"Thank you awfully," said Kitty, rising.

"Then, now, good night, dear. My room is quite close if you need me, and if ever you want a little chat with someone who understands most things, well, here I am," and Mrs. Webster gave the young girl a confidence-winning smile.

"Thank you," said Kitty. She was dismayed to find that her lip was quivering.

"I hope we kiss," and Mrs. Webster, put an arm about her.

But the feel of the motherly arms was too much for poor Kitty. To Mrs. Webster's consternation, she broke down in a dreadful fit of weeping.

"My dear child," said Mrs. Webster, as she drew Kitty down beside her on a sofa, "I fear that you are in real trouble."

"No, no, it is nothing!" gasped Kitty. "Only, nobody has ever kissed me since Mother died."

Then she broke down again, and Mrs. Webster waited patiently for her to recover herself.

"I don't suppose that your uncle would mind if you confided in me a little," she said at last. "So many people do, and I am quite safe."

Kitty raised her head.

"My uncle has nothing whatever to do with me now," she said hardly.

Mrs. Webster noticed the tone, and was wise enough to see that there was some temper mixed with the genuine sorrow.

"It would be such a very long story if I were to tell you everything," said Kitty more calmly; "and if I were only to tell you part, it would not be fair."

"There is no hurry, dear," said Mrs. Webster kindly.

"I think, perhaps, my mother would like me to tell you, because I really don't know what to do," said poor Kitty.

"I feel sure she would," said Mrs. Webster.

Kitty heaved another great sigh, as though she were trying to unload herself of all her emotion. Then she began at the very beginning and told, as honestly as she could, the story of the old life in London and the new life at Threlby End, finishing up with the astounding news about her father and the fortune that had come to her.

"So now, you see, Mrs. Webster," said Kitty in conclusion, "I really haven't a notion what I ought to do. I can't pretend that I don't want money—I want it frightfully—but it feels absolutely horrible to think of touching any of this money that has come from my father," and Kitty dropped her voice at the last word.

"I entirely understand your feeling," said Mrs. Webster warmly; "but now, dear, you and I must pull ourselves together, and try to look at life from a common-sense point of view. Feelings are very sacred things, but sometimes they come in the way of clear eyesight."

Kitty gave a slow nod of agreement, and waited for more.

"This money you speak of is in the hands of your guardian, and he will not be able to spend it except for your benefit. You must quietly take that fact as settled, and prepare to fall in with any plan your guardian may make. If you are not, as I gather, happy at Threlby End, it may be better for you to have a complete change. It really must be a very lonely place for any young girl——"

"But I loved it!" Kitty broke out unexpectedly.

"Oh, I am sorry, dear! From what you have just said I thought you hated the place."

Kitty gave a wan kind of smile.

"That is the queer part. I thought I hated it, but the minute Uncle Jonathan wanted to get rid of me I found that I loved it."

"I see!" and Mrs. Webster smiled kindly. "Well, Kitty, I feel sure that you have done right in telling me all this, and I should like to think things over. We must both sleep on all this and pray."

"I can't pray," said Kitty quickly.

"No, I thought you couldn't," said Mrs. Webster with a kind frankness. "I would tell your Father in heaven all about that, so that He may teach you how again."

Kitty threw up her arms and gave a hearty kiss to her new friend.

There came a tap at the door.

"Roddy and Tim!" exclaimed Mrs. Webster sternly, as she opened it.

Kitty saw two figures in striped and faded pyjamas, standing arm in arm, gazing at their mother with twinkling eyes; but she could not understand at first what they were talking about.

"We mayn't speak together, but we can't help thinking together. So we got out of bed together, and here we are together," said Roddy.

"But why?" Mrs. Webster's face relaxed to a smile.

"It's Don, Mother," said Tim. "The poor injured beast is howling fit to break a heart of iron."

"And she said"—and Roddy pointed at Kitty—"that he always slept on her bed at Threlby End; and we said that you would have a fit if she proposed such a thing here, and so we thought it was our Christian duty to come and explain for her."

"Would you really like the dog upstairs so very much, dear?" asked Mrs. Webster, though it was martyrdom indeed to think of any dog sleeping in the best visitors' room.

"He always does sleep with me," admitted Kitty.

"But not on the bed?"

"Oh no! I could make him lie on the mat," said Kitty eagerly. "He behaves like a perfect gentleman, and always does what I tell him."

"Very well, boys," sighed Mrs. Webster resignedly. "You can bring him up."

"And may we reckon that it is breakfast-time now?" asked Roddy, pressing his advantage.

"Oh, very well!" laughed his mother.

"There really is no discipline in this house," sighed Tim, as he looked into his mother's eyes.

In a minute or two there was a terrific scramble on the stairs, and Don came yelping into the room.

"I do believe that you will be all right now, Kitty," said Mrs. Webster, shaking her head mournfully.

"But do you mind dreadfully?" cried Kitty.

"I do—dreadfully! I never was an animal lover. I merely wish to be kind to them, poor things."

"Then thank you more than ever!" said Kitty gratefully.

"You should really thank us," cried Roddy. "Tim and I would have spent the night with racking headaches if that dog had howled on, and every lesson we had ever crammed up would have hooked it out of our brains."

"And Father and Mamma would have had to

pay for our keep in an idiot asylum for the rest of our lives," added Tim.

"It seems to me that Don has done it all by his own howling," laughed Kitty. And Don, standing on all-fours, with tail hard at work, looked with an impudent triumph at the party.

"Cut along, boys!" said their mother.

"Come, Mamma!" said Tim, and seizing his mother by one arm, while Roddy attacked the other, they led her off.

CHAPTER XXI

A Call on the Invalid

"HERE is a letter for you, dear," said Mrs. Webster, when Kitty returned from school on the following day.

"Thank you."

Kitty was not used to letters; but she could see that this was from her uncle.

She opened it as she stood there, and it did not take long to read.

"THE CLUB,
"HIGH RIGG.

"DEAR KATHERINE,

"I hear from your guardian, Mr. Marmaduke, that he would like to see you as soon as possible; so, as I am going to London next Monday, I should be glad if you would ask Mrs. Webster whether she will be so very kind as to arrange for you to meet me at High Rigg on that day. Come by your ordinary school train.

"Perhaps, also, she will be good enough to see that you are provided with anything she thinks you may need. Mr. Marmaduke has sent the enclosed cheque for your immediate use.

"Believe me,
"Your affectionate uncle,
"JONATHAN THRELBY."

Kitty unfolded the cheque with bewildered curiosity. It was for twenty pounds.

With a staggered expression on her face she handed the note and the cheque to her hostess.

"I see," said Mrs. Webster. "Well, I am sure that we can manage to get you off by Monday. As for clothes,"—and she puckered her forehead— "perhaps you ought to get a few little things——"

"You know I haven't a thing fit to wear, Mrs. Webster," said Kitty frankly, as she glanced down at her shabby skirt.

"That can soon be put right," the doctor's wife answered cheerfully. "Poor Nell, how she would love to help you to choose!"

"Nell?"

"Yes. Nell has a mania for clothes, and she has had many a snubbing from me and the boys about it. Still, if you really wish to do a Christian kindness to a poor invalid, consult Nell about your wardrobe. She will unearth bushels of fashion papers, and will choose the right designs for your particular style."

"How funny!" laughed Kitty.

"It is funny. But she has taste. I wonder— would you be hurt if I suggested something I have on my mind?"

"Oh no!" said Kitty rather anxiously.

"Well, dear, I have been thinking that you would feel more cheerful if you went out of mourning."

"Oh, I couldn't!" she exclaimed.

"I think you could. I believe that your mother would have agreed with me."

"Very well, Mrs. Webster," said Kitty with a most surprising meekness.

In this older lady's presence she was discovering that it was rather nice not to have any will of her own. For Kitty was tired of thinking and thinking for herself, and she had made up her mind with a great sense of relief that she would do exactly what Mrs. Webster advised in everything.

But twenty pounds! She had never had such a sum in her life, and it felt, indeed, as though she were handling a fortune.

But there was no time for further thought. The boys came rampaging home for tea, and afterwards they rushed off, by special invitation, to call on Nell before supper.

"The invalid doesn't exactly sound as though she were at death's door," said Tim in a low tone, as he and Roddy and Kitty crept up the stairs.

They could hear Nell's rippling laugh, but a gruff voice puzzled them.

"Who can she have with her?" whispered Roddy.

"Soon see," breathed Tim. "You knock," and he pushed Kitty forward.

Kitty tapped, and opened the door in reply to a gay "Come in!" and the three entered, followed by Don.

"Heaps of room!" said Nell, as she screwed her head round to look at them.

She was lying flat, her head and shoulders raised slightly on a mass of pillows.

She looked amazingly different from the usual

Nell, for she had persuaded Nurse to dress her fair hair high up on her head with combs and hairpins, on the plea that she wanted it out of the way, but really because she wanted to pretend to herself that she was an injured queen. She was wearing a sumptuous dressing-jacket, and the Suffrage colours were pinned on the sleeve which she could not use; but her face was awesomely white, and her blue eyes looked big and sunken, with dark shadows under them, and it was clear to all that poor Nell had really suffered.

But what astonished the visitors most was to see the burly blacksmith himself seated at the bedside, carefully watching the antics of a beautifully ugly bull pup, who was scrambling about on the pillows.

"I say, what a gem!" exclaimed Roddy, and, for- getting to greet Nell, he made a rush for the pup.

"Down, Don!" said Kitty hastily, and she snatched her own dog by the collar.

"Isn't he glorious?" cried Nell. "Look at his expression!" Then, as Roddy lifted him up and gazed at him covetously, she added: "Only, no bagging. He's mine! my own special darling!"

"Aye, I've brought him for a bit of company for her," said Gregory, "and he's quite agreeable, seemingly."

As for Don, having received a whispered scold- ing from his mistress, he pretended that he took not the remotest interest in the new-comer, and, jumping up on the window-seat, he gazed out into the road as though he were absorbed in looking for motor-cars.

The three visitors shook Nell's left hand effusively, asked how she was without waiting for the answer, and then looked round for seats.

"Perch yourselves high up," said Nell, "so that I can see you all."

So they ranged themselves in view of the prostrate invalid and proceeded to enjoy themselves.

"Nurse says that I may have you to supper if you can stay," said Nell to Kitty. "She can't be bothered with boys," and she darted a challenging look towards them.

"Where is the mighty giant, Nurse Samson?" asked Roddy. "We are simply dying to see her!"

"I am here!" said a voice.

They turned and looked towards a dressing-room door. The sight curiously upset them. The boys broke into irrepressible laughter.

"My hat!" breathed Tim.

For Nurse Samson turned out to be the tiniest and daintiest little woman ever seen in hospital cap and apron.

Nurse Samson enjoyed the joke with them, and shook hands cordially enough.

"She is a terror all the same!" said Nell ruefully; then, as the smith looked rather mystified, they shot explanations at him.

"Well, miss," he said, "it's often said that there is good stuff in little room—as there is in that there pup—and if you've got the job of keeping all this lot in their right places, well, there'll need to be!"

"You are a beastly traitor, Gregory! Why can't

you let Nurse Samson fancy she is in a dovecot?"
said Tim.

" I'm an honest man," he replied.

" And, by the way—yes—I see there is some
left," said Roddy as he stared hard at the smith's
massive head.

" Why, what's left?" he asked as he rose to take
leave.

" Just a hair or two. I thought you said that if
Nell had an accident you were going to tear it all
off?"

" What I say I'll do, I do—always!" the smith
said impressively; " but no good wife can bear to
see her husband's hair fly. Mine rubbed me with
some grand bottle stuff this morning, and it all
grew again!"

Then he wished Nell good night, poked at the
pup, received a harmless bite for his pains, and
took his departure.

As soon as he had gone, the boys and Nell fell to
more eager talk, to which Nurse Samson and Kitty
made amused listeners.

They roved at random from Florrie Gregory and
Polly Dennison to Suffragettes and Nimrod, and
so onwards to the more urgent excitement of the
coming Flower Show.

" It is on the first Saturday that ever is, Kitty,"
said Roddy. " And I'll tell you what! You ought
to enter some of your stuff. Everyone in Morley
has to send something, if it is only a radish!
Entries don't close till Thursday."

" But how can I? I have nothing to enter."

"Why, you must have heaps and heaps! What about gooseberries and currants, roses and pansies? There must be piles of jolly things in your splendid old garden. We could go over early on Saturday morning before breakfast and get them. Mr. M'Leod would lend us his car, perhaps, if we talked to him nicely."

"Why, of course," put in Nell.

"See!" and Roddy pulled out a grubby and much-creased catalogue from his pocket.

Kitty glanced down it, trying to feel a polite interest in what was apparently exciting them all so much.

"Don't you see," persisted Roddy, "the Flower Show is THE thing that matters in Morley, except Christmas!"

"But I shall be going away," said Kitty excusingly.

"Feeble!" said Roddy. "You know you don't go until Monday."

"Why, where are you going?" asked Nell quickly.

"To London."

"Oh, not to the Suffragette procession?" groaned Nell enviously.

Kitty laughed out.

"No, just on business. My uncle wants me to go."

"It's really just a trick to miss school," said Tim gently. "The sort of thing girls do."

"That is it," said Kitty, anxious not to draw down upon herself further questions. "Marjory certainly did say that our black and red currants were splendid this season."

"Then we'll stick 'em down!" said Roddy, pulling out his pencil. "Anything else?"

"We've lettuces—beauties!"

And in the end Kitty found herself committed to six entries, and it was arranged that somehow or other the stuff must be got from Threlby End before the Show opened.

"Sorry to be disagreeable, friends," said Nurse, "but the patient must now subside for supper."

"Mean it?" asked Tim testily.

"Good night, boys. I shall be pleased to see you again to-morrow," was the answer.

"There is no doubt that Samson must have been able to kill a thousand Philistines with the jawbone of an ass," ruminated Tim as he rose to go.

"What are you going to call the pup?" asked Roddy as he gave it one last fondle.

"Cerberus, the darling!" said Nell. "He is guarding me from the gates of Death!"

"Go, please!" said Nurse Samson.

And they went.

At least the others thought so, but a minute later Tim poked his head into the room and remarked, in an ominous tone:

"I say, Nell, look out!"

"Why?" she called.

"Don't get fat!"

CHAPTER XXII

About Clothes and Other Things

Now, though Nell dearly loved a sparring match with the boys, it was delightful to get a real girl all to herself, so, during the picnic supper, Kitty, anxious to be kind, did her best to entertain her by telling her the ins and outs of real school life and little tantalizing bits about Threlby End.

As Mrs. Webster had warned Kitty, it was not long before Nell worked the conversation round to clothes. The London visit came up, and Kitty, putting her own feelings aside, admitted that if she went up with her uncle she must have something fit to wear.

"Mrs. Webster thinks that I ought to go out of mourning," she said seriously, "so I suppose I shall have to do it."

"Everyone does what Madam Dear says," admitted Nell. "She is such a firm, determined kind of dear that you can't help it."

"My uncle has sent me a cheque," continued Kitty, "so I suppose I shall have to spend some of it."

Nell sprang at the bait like a hungry trout.

"Oh, do tell me what you are going to get?"

"Haven't a notion.   It doesn't really matter."

"But it does," remonstrated Nell eagerly.   "It matters frightfully, because——"

"Go on.   I shan't be offended."

"I wasn't going to dream of offending you.   I was going to say that you are so jolly beautiful. Not just pretty, like me, but absolutely beautiful! I would give anything for your face—the shape of it and the colour of it and the softness of it!"

"No one has ever envied me my face before," laughed Kitty, flushing.

So the girls' tongues went full swing on clothes, until stopped by the entrance of Nell's father.

"Why, where is my daughter?" and he gazed about the room.

"Oh, my hair, you mean!" laughed Nell.   "Isn't it sweet?"

"I like my usual little girl best," he said as he stooped to kiss her.   "But what, in the name of wonder, is that thing?"

"Cerberus.   Isn't he precious, Dad? He's lying there guarding me from the gates of Death!"

"Really?"   Mr. M'Leod poked his finger under the drowsy puppy's chin.   "Hum! Exquisite! And how large does it get before it's done?"

"You are a horrible, uninteresting parent!" grumbled Nell.   "Sit down and tell me every single thing that has happened."

Mr. M'Leod seated himself, and, taking Nell's hand in his, he did his best to follow out her command.

Kitty felt it a strange kind of privilege to hear

a daughter talk to a father, yet, as she listened, her heart grew rather miserable, and she wondered whether she ought to slip away.

But Nell's father drew her pleasantly into the conversation, and after a while he left the room and returned with a heavy parcel.

"I know I oughtn't to indulge your depraved tastes, Nell, but I thought that perhaps these might keep you quiet."

His daughter watched eagerly as he undid the package, but her countenance fell when he produced two dull-looking books.

But when she opened one of them she uttered a squeal of pure joy, and her father was completely satisfied; for the books contained rare plates of exquisitely gowned folk of all degrees, from far back in the centuries.

Nell was nearly beside herself with pleasure, and Kitty came nearer that she might see.

"Daddy, it is perfectly ripping of you!" she cried. "They must have cost a fortune!"

"They did. But I calculated that you would not want any new clothes for such a long time!"

"N—o!" said Nell dubiously. "But Kitty does! She is going to London next week, and we have been deciding on her clothes."

"Then you will have been quite happy. Sorry I interrupted," he laughed; then he added: "Kitty, I don't seem to treat you as a visitor. I can't, after what you did for my little girl."

"He will call me his 'little girl' until I am twenty," pouted Nell. "Oh, must you really go?"

" I shall get into a row if I don't just skip through some of my lessons," said Kitty, rising.

"Oh, well, if you do get a rowing, come in to-morrow and tell me what they said! I wonder what I shall feel like when I get into a row at school."

Nell spoke as though she rather looked forward to the possibility.

"You will be as meek as a scared rabbit!" chuckled her father.   He rose and opened the door for Kitty, just as though she had been grown-up. "You won't forsake my little girl after all your kindness to her, will you?" he said kindly.

" I won't," said Kitty happily, as she smiled up at him.

CHAPTER XXIII
Two Blows At Once

WHEN Kitty reached school on the following morning Miss Mason sent for her, and, with what kindness she could, broke it to her that she had failed in her examination.

"I cannot think what happened, dear," she said. "I am afraid that all along you have been too anxious."

"I am just stupid," said Kitty, trying to put a bold face on her trouble.

"No, you are not stupid," her mistress answered. "It is very disappointing for you, but we must see what other openings we can find."

"Thank you," said Kitty nervously, and after a few moments of rather awkward talk, Kitty left Miss Mason's sanctum.

Oh dear! Though Kitty had been practically certain that she had failed, she knew as she walked along the corridor that her heart was thumping horribly, now that Miss Mason had quenched the last spark of lingering hope.

How much simpler it would have been if she could have told her uncle that she had won the scholarship, and that she wished to go right off to the beautiful seaside college!

The girls came up in a rush to condole with her, and their sympathy was cheering in its way; but the worst of it was that she had to do her best to be jolly and congratulate the "freckly one", who had succeeded at the head of the list.

Altogether Kitty felt very cheap that morning, and, as it was a tennis afternoon, she excused herself early and left the school, deciding that she would like to go off somewhere and bury herself.

As there was plenty of time for the train, she sauntered along the Station Road absently, intent on killing time, which seemed of no importance on this sunny afternoon.

But as she passed her eye over a great hoarding of brilliant advertisements she was startled to very sharp attention and stood stock-still, oblivious of everything that passed around her.

The poster which attracted her attention read as follows:—

THRELBY END, BOAR FELL, MORLEY

Messrs. Rutter & Bland have received instructions from Jonathan Threlby, Esq., J.P., to sell by auction at the "Black Bull", High Rigg, on 10th July:

All those valuable properties known as Threlby End, Boar Fell, and Morley.

The lands, woods, Mansion, and cottages will be sold without reserve.

Plans, surveys, and further particulars can be obtained from Messrs. Taggart & Taggart on application.

AT THRELBY END

Will be SOLD, the entire contents of the above residence; including valuable antique and modern furniture, pictures, plate, ornaments, curios, books, china, and all other indoor and outdoor effects.

On VIEW for three days before the commencement of the Sale.

Detailed Catalogues will be issued shortly, and may be had on application from the Auctioneers.

To say that Kitty's breath was taken away would be to put it mildly indeed.

She read and re-read the placard, feeling as though the words flamed and blinded her eyes; then walked slowly along in the direction of the station, and never even noticed that a man darted a curious look at her as he passed.

What could all this mean? Where was Uncle Jonathan going to live?

She began to hurry, hardly knowing what she did, and suddenly in front of her she caught sight of a familiar figure.

Uncle Jonathan! She would have known him anywhere by the stoop of his shoulders.

Why should she not run up to him and ask what all this meant?

That would have been the simple thing for a niece to do. But an evil spirit rose in Kitty. Uncle Jonathan must have been planning this for ages. He ought to have told her himself. It was monstrous that she should see the news first on a public notice-board. Her uncle had deliberately deceived her. So she argued bitterly. She darted down a narrow entry, so that she might take a short cut to the station and escape, and, having half an hour to wait, she crossed the line and secluded herself in a field, so that she might think in peace.

Now Roddy had come to High Rigg that morning on a visit to the dentist, and he had promised to look out for her; but even Roddy's cheerful company would be troublesome just now.

As she gazed across the field the hot air seemed to dance over the brilliant grass which was springing up so gaily now that the hay had been taken.

As her first anger cooled, a dreadful feeling was coming over Kitty that perhaps she had made a mistake, and that Uncle Jonathan was really very poor after all.

She began to remember that Uncle Jonathan had looked wretched when last they had spoken together, and she began to regret that she had not run after him and been nice to him.

But it was too late to think of that now, and at last she looked across towards the railway and was startled to see that the signal was down.

Kitty leaped up and rushed off to the train, and as she reached the platform she saw Roddy waving frantically at her.

"I say! You've cut it fine. Where on earth have you been?" he demanded, as he banged the door.

"I was sitting in a field, and I clean forgot the time."

"Oh!" he looked at her intently.

"Did you have a very horrible business?" she asked.

"Dentist? No, that was all right. He pottered about in the usual style and kept me waiting ages." Roddy spoke as though he was not thinking about the dentist. He was clearly excited about something, and Kitty waited for him to explain.

"Why ever didn't you tell us?" he asked, planting himself down in front of her and leaning forward.

"Tell you what?"

"Don't pretend you don't know!"

"How could I tell you what I didn't know myself?"

Roddy gave a low whistle.

"Is that a positive fact?"

"I only tell lies occasionally."

"Wasn't it rather rough luck?" he asked sympathetically.

"I am used to rough luck. I have failed in the exam too!"

"You haven't!"

"I tell you I don't lie, usually," and she gave a forced laugh.

Roddy's usual readiness failed him, and he stumped to the far window and banged it down, merely to relieve his feelings and fill up the time.

"I am sorry I have got the hump," said Kitty. "They call me Kitty Up-and-Down at school. I am Down just now, and I don't want to bother you with all my bothers."

"It's tremendously jolly to be bothered!" said Roddy anxiously. "Do you know, when I read that poster I was such a beast! I forgot all about how it would feel to you. I simply gloated over the idea that we could get the Scheme through now."

"Why, so you can. I never thought of that. How splendid!"

But Kitty's voice sounded terribly unnatural, as though she were not thinking what she was saying, and presently she startled the boy by remarking:

"I am going to get out at Boarside and walk round by Boar Fell to Morley. I simply must see the place again before the horrible public come poking round and spoiling it for ever!"

"But you can't possibly do that!" exclaimed Roddy.

"Why can't I? Eight or nine miles is nothing to me. I have been used to letting my own legs carry me about."

"I don't believe Mother would like it," he contended.

"I am quite sure she wouldn't. But I must!"

"Why must you?"

"Because—can't you see how outrageous it was of Uncle Jonathan to get me quietly out of the way and do a thing like this? I must see Threlby End again! How he can——" Kitty shrugged her shoulders with a despairing action.

"Look here," said Roddy. "That's all right, but do have a little sense! Mother will perfectly understand that you will want to go back to get your own possessions, and she'll motor you over. You may honestly depend on that."

But an obstinate expression gripped Kitty's mouth. She did not want to go for the last tour of inspection of her lost home even with Mrs. Webster. She wanted to be quite alone and indulge in a good old mope.

"It is no use arguing," she said firmly. "I have absolutely made up my mind. You can go on to Morley and explain. I shall be there easily by nine o'clock."

"You mustn't really!" he urged.

"You can't stop me," she said, with a laugh. "Besides, how do you know that I don't want to find out whether there is anything in the garden fit for your Flower Show?"

"A rotten excuse! Of course I can understand that you are pretty sick about the place being sold; but being sick about something doesn't make it any righter to do wrong."

"I'll take all the blame and all the responsibility," said Kitty perversely. "And afterwards, if your mother wants me to clear out—well, I suppose there is always the workhouse for waifs and strays like me!"

"Kitty! You have no right to talk like that," said Roddy angrily. Then, pulling himself together, he added: "I say, don't!"

"I really must. If you like to take my books for me I shall be obliged. Not but what I am used to lugging them for miles."

"Go your own way, then," said Roddy. His

tone was decidedly cross. Girls were so frightfully obstinate, and you never could be sure what they would think of doing next; and the worst of it was that you couldn't punch their heads to put the sense into them.

Having disagreed, the two dropped all conversation, and Roddy leaned far out of the window and tried to soothe his mind by whistling "The British Grenadiers".

When the train slowed down at Boarside, Kitty darted a look at the boy; then, as he had not taken any notice of her suggestion about the books, she hoisted her bag on her shoulder and got out.

"I'll really be at Morley by nine," she remarked as she turned off.

"As you like!" he replied, and at his tone Kitty gave a toss of her head and hurried off. She didn't quite approve of being snubbed by a mere boy.

Roddy waited until the train was just on the move, then he opened the door and jumped out.

Kitty had already left the station, but on catching her up he laid a heavy hand on her shoulder.

CHAPTER XXIV

The Find

KITTY started back with a cry, which Roddy answered with an insulting laugh.

"Roddy, how dare you!"

"You didn't think I would let you go alone?" he asked doggedly. "You'll have to make the best of me, Miss Katherine Threlby. I'll walk six yards behind you if you like; I've done that often when Tim is on the grump; but I won't lose sight of you—no, not if you run like a stoat. I can be just as pig-headed as any girl when I choose."

Kitty looked hard at him, and to tell the truth she wanted to laugh.

"But now you will get into a row too."

"I know my way about in rows. Besides, I should get into a far worse one if I were to let you go over the hills and far away on your own. Girls were only made to drag men about after them," and he sighed.

"But it is too stupid of you," exclaimed Kitty. "Now Mrs. Webster will worry when neither of us turn up."

"Oh no, Mother won't worry! She may rage a bit. She'll only think we have lost the train. She hates that kind of thing, and we shall have to be sure to get home before the late train arrives, or—well, then I won't exactly answer for things."

"All right, I can walk awfully quickly," said Kitty.

She was not exactly repenting, but she was certainly feeling a trifle anxious.

"Go on ahead, then!" Roddy stood still. "Guess your six yards and I'll keep my distance."

"Don't be absurd," laughed Kitty. "Now that I have dragged you into this we might as well be civil."

Obviously the best thing to do now was to step out at a good spanking pace, and though Kitty had meant to notice every detail of the dear old road as she passed over it for the last time, it was impossible to be sentimental with Roddy striking in with all kinds of odd remarks.

On the whole, Kitty was glad. The idea of this adventure had taken her suddenly, and she was not sorry to have Roddy's gay companionship.

"Who is that old witch?" he asked, as they came in sight of Belle leaning over her gate. "I don't fancy her."

But at sight of Kitty, Belle rushed out into the road with more than her usual excitement.

"Oh, my darling! My darling Miss Kitty! I've waited for two long days for the sight of your sweet face! I thought you were ill! I thought you were dead! Yet here you are, fresh as the morning, with as fine a young gentleman——"

"What is all that tommy-rot?" asked Roddy, aside to Kitty. "Is she dotty?"

But Kitty scowled at him, and, taking Belle's hand, she said:

"No, no, Belle, I am all right. I am staying at Morley. Threlby End is shut up."

"Ah!" said Belle, with a weird laugh. "Then it's true."

"Come on!" said Roddy disgustedly, dragging at Kitty's arm.

"No, no, young master! Don't you be in such a hurry! Spare a moment for a lonely old body who never sees a friendly face, never hears a kind word, never——"

"Just a minute, Roddy," whispered Kitty. "But what have you heard, Belle?"

"I've heard what I have heard, Miss Kitty. Ah, well, judgment waits and judgments come, and them that can only spare a threepenny bit to a lone widow woman—well, they'll have taken from them what they have."

"Considering that you never see anybody and never hear anybody, it's queer to think that you have got hold of any news," sneered Roddy as he kept hold of Kitty.

"Ah, young gentleman," she whined, "but the luck came to me to-day! It did for sure. As sweet a young lady as ever wore shoe leather leaned over that fence, not an hour ago. She was a tourist, and was looking out for grand scenery and old houses and such-like. I showed her mine, and then I told her that if she wanted a better spot, she'd better get over the fell to Threlby End. And she had money too!" and Belle displayed a bright half-crown in triumph.

"I suppose the money found the way to your heart," chaffed Roddy.

"Money finds its way into most people's hearts, my lad," said the woman tartly. "But there's more than money poor Belle got. She got a smile and a kind word. I told her something besides. I told her how the Squire of Threlby End was the talk of the countryside, of how he was that mean that——"

"Belle!" exclaimed Kitty, feeling very uncomfortable. "How could you say such a thing?"

"The way he treats you, my beautiful darling, is enough for old Belle. He's spited you and he's spited me, and I'll spite him. That is the only way in the world. An eye for an eye, and a tooth for a tooth, as the blessed Bible says!" and Belle clapped her hands and gave a foolish spring in the air.

"She's absolutely dotty," whispered Roddy. "Do come on!"

And Kitty came, for she was rather glad to be dragged out of reach of the old woman's evil tongue.

"How on earth did you ever get on speaking terms with such an old creature?" he asked.

"Easily enough. She's a poor old thing living alone in that disgraceful house, and as I pass twice a day she has got into the way of looking out for me. I take her little things sometimes, and I believe I am her only bit of real pleasure."

"But she's dotty," said Roddy, "and I don't believe she is safe."

"There's no real harm in her, but I should be dotty myself if I lived as she does."

But Belle was not an interesting topic, and, as they left the broader road for the western fell, Kitty began telling Roddy stories of Don's sagacity. From dogs they turned to horses, and before Kitty realized what she was doing she had confided to the boy her passion for horses, and given him some idea of her strange life at the riding-school.

"This place feels jolly weird," said Roddy, as at last they walked up the drive. "I rather wonder that you ever managed to live here for a whole year."

"I rather wonder myself. But you get to love a place when you have nothing else to love."

"Do you?"

"But we mustn't dawdle. We had better go round the garden and see if there is anything fit for the Flower Show, and afterwards we can go through the house."

"But how can we, when it is locked up?"

"I know how to get in—that is, if you can climb."

"Climb! But I wonder that Mr. Threlby leaves this place all by itself without any caretaker."

"Oh, well, Samuel potters round, and all the valuables are sent away! Nobody wants to steal furniture and carpets and pots and pokers."

"No," said Roddy dubiously.

"Why," and Kitty smiled, "Marjory and I have been left alone in the house, and anybody could have got in and put pistols to our heads and grabbed at everything they wanted."

"But you had Don."

"Don would certainly not have left much of anyone who had tried to interfere with us," Kitty admitted; "but we are really so far out of the world that people don't even bother to steal the fruit. In fact, I believe that everyone has forgotten all about us."

"Well, let's see what your garden grows," said Roddy. So they wandered about the desolate garden, which was only cultivated in odd bits; but they found what they wanted, and Roddy declared that six entries would be easily collected.

"We'll come before breakfast on Saturday morning and gather the stuff," he decided.

They feasted merrily on fruit, and lettuces which they washed at the pump, and then, as the sun was setting all too quickly, Kitty offered to show Roddy the way into the house.

She led him along the terrace to the west front, round to the south wing, and pointed out to him a straggling plum-tree which grew against a low annexe, once a garden-house.

"We can climb up there, and over the roof, and in at the passage window," said Kitty. "I've done it before, when I have come back before my usual time and found Marjory out. I know that the latch of the window is broken."

The climbing was easy enough, and, as Kitty had foreseen, the window opened without any trouble and they got through into the empty house.

"If you would rather wander round alone I will stay here," said Roddy tactfully.

"Rather not. I should loathe to be alone now," said Kitty cheerfully. "Besides, I'd love to show you things."

So they skirmished through the house, and in their eagerness they quite ignored the time and gave themselves up to enjoyment.

"I simply can't conceive how Mr. Threlby can endure to sell all these things," said Roddy.

They were standing in the drawing-room, and Kitty pulled back one of the heavy blinds.

"Who is that beautiful woman?" asked the boy.

"That is Mrs. Threlby—my Aunt Molly. She was killed, you know."

Roddy nodded and stared up into the gay eyes of the sportswoman.

"She's beautiful—very. It was a great pity!"

"Yes," said Kitty.

"You know, she makes me feel rather a beast. I've said such nasty things against your uncle. That's the worst of saying nasty things—you nearly always have to back out afterwards."

"Yes," said Kitty, thinking of what her own mother had once said to her.

"Perhaps it really is true that Mr. Threlby shut up most of his house because his heart was broken. We thought it was bosh."

This time Kitty did not speak.

"People do that sort of thing sometimes, so I've heard," went on Roddy.

But Kitty suddenly clutched at Roddy's arm.

"Roddy! There was someone looking in!"

The two rushed to the window. They peered

out, but there was no one to be seen on the empty terrace. Only the great red sun glared at them from away over Boar Fell.

"Let's open the window!" cried Roddy.

"Oh no!" Kitty laughed nervously. "I'm a silly idiot. I thought for just a second that Uncle Jonathan had come back," and she drew the blind across.

"We really ought to be starting for Morley," said Roddy anxiously.

"Yes," Kitty agreed. "I just want to get one or two little things from my room. I won't be a jiff!"

"Then don't let it be a girl's jiff," laughed Roddy, as they went upstairs to the landing. "I'll wait by the window."

Roddy was impatiently thinking that Kitty's jiff was going to be of the usual feminine kind, when he was startled by noticing a movement from behind some shrubs on his left.

Surely someone was stirring?

He leaned farther out, and there, large as life, he saw the figure of a young lady pass into a narrow path between overgrown beech hedges.

"Hallo!" he shouted.

But there was no reply, and, turning, Roddy called out "Kitty!"

"Coming!" she answered him. She came flying along the passage with a face aglow with excitement.

"Kitty! You were right! There was someone! I've just seen her; she's behind that beech hedge."

" But who?"

" Haven't a notion!"

" I know," said Kitty bitterly. " Some wretched bit of the public poking round. But, Roddy, look here!"

In the passage darkness he could not see clearly what she held out to him, so she dragged him to the window and showed him a leather case in which there lay a superb pearl and diamond necklace.

"I say! Jolly fine! I didn't know you had anything as decent as that!" he blurted out.

" Nor did I," she laughed nervously. " But you don't understand. I was looking in my drawer for some ribbon and I found it."

" But who can have put it there?"

" Uncle Jonathan. There's no one else. Besides, read that."

Roddy took a slip of paper and read:

" To Katherine. This necklace was my wedding gift to your Aunt Molly. I would like you to have it. Uncle Jonathan."

Roddy was silent for a moment or two; then he said solemnly:

"I say! That's a big thing to have done—don't you think?"

" I don't know what to think," said Kitty gravely, as she closed up the case.

" It's getting jolly gloomy," suggested Roddy.

Kitty nodded, ran back to her room for one or two trifles she needed, stuffed them into her school bag, and then she and Roddy climbed down through the window and hurried off.

CHAPTER XXV
Morley Hears the News

THAT evening Morley seethed with excitement.

The poster announcing the property sale had been read and re-read, and it was amazing to hear the variety of reasons which were given as to why Mr. Threlby should be clearing out from the district in this drastic way.

"Aye, well," said the smith to a little group of villagers, "it's an ill wind that blows nobody any good. We'll like get Morley Model Village Scheme through after all."

Tim had returned from school on Hop, riding at as rough a pace as Nell had ever been guilty of, and had poured out all the news to his mother.

"I wonder what poor Kitty will think," said Mrs. Webster. "It will be a great shock to her, I expect."

"She's queer, is Kitty," admitted Tim. "You can't quite add her up, somehow."

Mr. M'Leod came to The Warren after supper, and he and the doctor and his wife had a tremendous Scheme talk from the new point of view, to which Tim listened with grave but obvious joy.

"Father," he broke in at last, "haven't you a ghost of a notion why Mr. Threlby is selling?"

"I have a notion, and it is certainly rather

ghostly. I heard on my rounds that he was going off to Canada. If that is so, he naturally wishes to realize his property."

"And will he leave Kitty on the parish?"

"Kitty is not exactly on the parish. But, as I happen to know something of Kitty's private affairs, we won't discuss her," answered his mother.

"I wonder why they have missed the train," said Tim. "Perhaps Mr. Threlby has met them at High Rigg and stuck to them."

"Great minds agree," said his mother. "Exactly what I was thinking."

"My poor little girl is all on the rampage to see Kitty before she settles for the night," struck in Mr. M'Leod, "and I have promised to try to prevail on a certain stern lady to allow her to come, if only for three minutes."

"How you can expect such a nurse as Nurse Samson to stay with a patient and parent who break every rule of sickness passes my comprehension."

"Nell would demoralize anyone, Mamma," said Tim.

"Nell ought to collapse behind closed blinds at nine o'clock," said Mrs. Webster with an attempt at sternness.

"But on such a sweet evening?" remonstrated Nell's father.

"Hallo! Here are the wanderers!" cried Tim, as two figures hurried past the window.

A moment more and the door opened, and there they truly were, hot, flushed, and very dusty.

Kitty and Roddy looked decidedly outfaced at

finding the "whole collection" sitting there, and Kitty came forward anxiously.

"I am so sorry, Mrs. Webster," she apologized. "It was all my doing. I would get out, and then Roddy thought it was his duty to stick to me."

"But you got out where, my dear child?"

"At Boarside. I heard some news — perhaps you have all heard it too?" and she looked round.

"Rather!" said Tim emphatically.

"So "—she dropped her voice—" I wanted to see Threlby End once more—before anybody spoiled it!"

"You mean, dear, that you two have walked all the way round by Threlby End from Boarside Station?" asked Mrs. Webster incredulously.

"It was only about nine miles—we aren't a scrap tired," Kitty insisted.

"No, not a bit, really!" said Roddy.

"If ever I saw a fagged-out couple I see that couple now," put in the doctor. "Did you give her anything to eat, Roddy?"

"We have had fruit and lettuces."

"Come along this moment and let us see what we can find!" exclaimed Mrs. Webster.

"It really wasn't Roddy's fault!" urged Kitty, as she followed her hostess into the dining-room. "I got out. I was mad to get out, and he tried to stop me. Then he got out too. He wouldn't let me go alone."

"I couldn't possibly have let her cut along by herself, could I, Mother?"

"Not possibly."

And at his mother's words, and the look she gave him, a burden rolled away.

"You've missed an awfully exciting talk about the Scheme," said Tim as he joined them. "We've practically settled everything."

"The Scheme will keep, dear," said his mother pointedly. "We want to hear the adventures of the latest arrivals."

Now during the long walk home Kitty and Roddy had chummed up amazingly, and Kitty had found herself telling the boy all sorts of things. But Roddy was so sympathetic, and so frankly anxious to hear, and looked at things from such a refreshingly new view-point, that his criticisms had done her good.

Little by little she had been drawn to tell him of the old home life in London, of her father, and how he had left her mother and herself to fight the battle of life for themselves, and of the fortune that had so strangely come into her hands.

It all sounded to Roddy like some unreal fairy tale, but it was interesting to hear the princess's troubles at first hand from the princess herself.

Roddy was the principal speaker at the supper table, and it was after he had finished that Kitty, noticing that he had tactfully left out part of the story, drew a leather case from her blouse and told them about this great surprise.

"My dear child! How lovely it is!" said Mrs. Webster.

"I can't wear it, of course," said Kitty. "It is far too grown-up."

"You must wear it on your eighteenth birthday," said Mrs. Webster cheerfully.

"Only, where shall I be then?" sighed Kitty.

"It must be awfully queer not to be able to imagine what comes next," said Tim thoughtfully.

"Oh, Tim," exclaimed Kitty, as she suddenly remembered something, "you were right after all in choosing the 'freckly one'! She got the scholarship, and I failed, like a dunce."

"I say! I'm awfully sorry!"

"Yes. Poor Roddy!" said Kitty. "He bears up well."

"I chose you as my champion, and you are my champion," said Roddy stoutly. "Besides, who cares for exams?"

"Dear, I forgot," exclaimed Mrs. Webster. "Nell wants you to go over and say 'good night'; but are you too tired?"

"Not a bit," said Kitty, jumping up.

"And you must let Nell see this," said Tim, as he closed the case. "She will simply squirm with envy."

"She needn't. She has——"

But Kitty stopped herself and ran off.

When she had safely gone, the boys dawdled so that they might talk everything over again with their mother.

"It is so funny to think that Kitty is a kind of a golden nugget after all," said Tim.

"Yes. I am sorry for her—very! But if everyone tries to act sensibly I trust that things will come right in the end," said Mrs. Webster thoughtfully.

CHAPTER XXVI
Round the Corner

It was on the following Friday night that Roddy "bagged" Cook's alarm-clock, so that he might set it for five o'clock.

He sprang up in a fright when the horrible thing went off, and then ran along a passage and tapped at Kitty's door.

The occasion was important, for it had been decided that Tim should stay on duty at the Flower Show, but that Roddy and Kitty should ride over to Threlby End to see what they could find.

Kitty was wild with excitement, for she had borrowed a makeshift rig from Nell and was to ride on Hop, Tim's horse.

Nell had pleaded to be waked that she might see them start, but Nurse Samson squashed the idea with vigour.

It was, happily, true that Nell was much better, for she had been out in the garden, and, though she could only sit up for a little, plans had been made to borrow a real Bath chair and take her to the Flower Show.

Now, on Flower Show day there was always a large garden-party at The Warren. By this annual invitation Mrs. Webster secured a big entry for the show, and rewarded the grandees for their patronage by giving them a sumptuous tea in her garden afterwards.

The day was therefore to be a busy and an exciting one, and, the night before, Nell had had the joy of seeing Kitty dressed in the sweetest white silk frock. It had been bought new for the occasion, and also for wear on any hot days there might be, when Kitty went up to London with her uncle.

It was sheer joy indeed for the two to trot along the road on that delicious morning. Kitty proved to Roddy that she knew her way about on a horse, while Don proved that it would have been an insult to leave him behind.

When within about a quarter of a mile of their journey's end, they passed the charcoal-burner's cottage.

The man was out in his shirt-sleeves, grooming his old horse and puffing at his pipe.

At the sound of the hoofs he raised his eyes.

"Hallo, Mr. Birkett!" called Roddy.

"Good morning!" said the man in a surprised tone. "And what gets gentlefolks up at this time o' day?"

"The point is, have you ever heard of Morley and District Flower Show?"

"Have I ever heard of t' Fell yonder?" answered the old man.

"Well, this lady here is going to sweep the decks with red currants, lettuces, gooseberries, peas, black currants, and pansies."

Kitty nodded and gave a gay laugh as she leaned down to stroke Hop's neck.

"Never have known you, miss, and that's the honest truth," said the charcoal-burner. "But, if your tale is true, you're doing a nasty trick by the birds."

"Bless their greedy little hearts!" laughed Roddy. "We'll show you the plunder when we come back," and away they went.

"Birkett can't surely be burning charcoal in July," exclaimed Roddy. "Isn't there a smell of burning?"

They sniffed suspiciously, and then with one accord touched their horses with their whips and dashed forward.

Every instant the scent of burning increased.

"Why, look there!" cried Kitty. She pointed over the tree-tops to the left of the road, where a column of dark-grey smoke rolled upwards.

Another fifty yards and they rounded a corner at a breakneck pace. From this point they ought to see the gardens and the roofs of Threlby End.

"Roddy!" Kitty's voice rang forth in a wail of consternation.

Another fifty yards. The grey column rose peacefully into the morning sunshine, but of Threlby End there was little to be seen.

"The place is burned down!" cried Roddy in a stunned kind of voice.

"Yes," said Kitty.

The gate was open. They galloped up the drive,

and half-way up Kitty reined in, flung herself off her horse, and put the rein about the branch of a tree.

Roddy followed her lead, and they turned up a path to the right, which led them into the rose garden.

There they stood together by the old sundial, silent with sheer amazement.

Some of the walls were standing, but the windows looked like awful eye-sockets from which the eyes had been gouged, and the roofs had entirely fallen in. No flames were to be seen, nothing but the quiet, lazy smoke. The fire had evidently finished its fearful work, and, like an evil giant, was sinking down to sleep off its gluttony.

"We must get nearer," exclaimed Kitty, breaking the spell which had fallen upon them. "Everything can't be gone!"

She darted off, and Roddy followed her, while Don shook his head and snorted in an important kind of way, looking up at his mistress as though to ask how she could possibly have allowed such an extraordinary thing to happen.

"Be careful you don't go too near, Kitty," called Roddy warningly. "Those walls might fall any moment."

The terrace was indeed littered with debris, and they soon saw that all the south end of the place was entirely burnt out, and only charred wood and burnt bricks remained of the garden-house.

"Let's get round to the back," said Kitty, vainly hoping that all was not gone.

They rushed round into the stable-yard, but from this side also the ruin was complete.

The hopeless extent of the catastrophe took from them all coherent language.

"I don't even see that it is any use to send for the fire-engine," said Kitty despairingly.

"I don't know that," said Roddy. "I think I had better gallop off to the village. The police will want to know the 'reason why' of this at any rate."

"And I ought to telegraph to Uncle Jonathan," said Kitty.

What would her uncle say?

"Have you his address?"

"The Club will find him."

"When you think that all those lovely things we saw on Wednesday are snuffed out to cinders," said Roddy, "it's simply fiendish!"

"They told us at school yesterday that nothing was ever really destroyed, but only resolved into its natural elements," said Kitty mockingly. "Have you a pencil and paper?"

Yes, Roddy could supply these in the form of a dirty envelope and an old stump; also he produced sixpence-halfpenny.

"You can write thirteen words."

"Yes, Grandmother!" agreed Kitty. "I'll write it; and then if you will go I'll stay."

"But need you stay?"

"I must wait for Uncle Jonathan, of course," she said decidedly; "besides, I can't let the poor old ruin die all by itself, can I, Don?"

The dog licked her hand sympathetically, quite

unable to understand this latest foolishness of mankind.

"Why, Samuel!"

The man came up at a lumbering trot, and stood stock-still, gasping at sight of the ruin and the excited boy and girl.

"Oh, there is Samuel! He can go," exclaimed Kitty, "if you don't mind him riding one of the horses?"

"Rather not," said Roddy. "That will be far the best, and then I can stay with you."

So Samuel was given his directions, and Kitty and Roddy remained to watch the ascending smoke as though they were magically fascinated.

"It is so extraordinary that no one spotted it until it got to this," said Roddy at last.

"Oh, well, I don't know about that!" said the girl. "You see, if it started burning at night, it might burn for hours without anyone being the wiser. There isn't a house for miles, except Birkett's, and his place is right on the other side of the copsewood."

"And sleeping like a dormouse, I'll wager," said Roddy. "But I don't see how it could start at night, with not a soul sleeping here."

"One can hardly think," mused Kitty, "that it was done by chance—it's so complete!"

"Kitty!" gasped Roddy. "What about that female we saw prowling round the other day? Suffragettes! That's it! I say! What a newspaper sensation!"

"Oh, but they couldn't!" cried Kitty.

"The Cause, you know," answered Roddy. "What a score! This will be a settler for Nell."

"But you aren't sure. You have no proof," said Kitty, frowning. "Perhaps it was an accident; a tramp may have been sleeping out, or something like that. Let's spy about. We may find matches or tobacco ash."

"Or hairpins," laughed Roddy. "We'll do a bit of Sherlocking," and they turned right about, for really it was necessary to do something.

"Here is some straw dragged across the yard," exclaimed Roddy, as he looked round.

"Stables," said Kitty.

The stables were intact, and they pushed the door open and entered.

"Hallo! Here we are!" said Roddy in a sepulchral voice. Yes, here was something, certainly.

Stuck up on the door of the loose-box there was a dirty piece of paper on which something was scrawled in printing letters. It was so illegible, however, that they had to take it into the daylight before they could make it out.

"ha ha ha mr Threlby. threpunce! threepunce! threepunce! ha ha ha."

"What in the earthly world can that mean?" demanded Roddy, after he had managed to read it aloud.

Then an idea seized him. It seized Kitty at the same time, and the two looked at one another in consternation.

"Belle!" gasped Kitty.

"I told you that she was mad," said Roddy.

But Kitty seized him by the arm as though she must hold on to him for support.

"Why, what is it?" For Kitty had gone as white as paper.

"What shall I do?" she gasped. "What shall I do?" and she shook his arm.

"Do?" he asked in astonishment. "Don't paralyse my arm anyway." Then, seeing that something really was the matter, he said kindly: "Why, what do you mean?"

"Don't you see?" she stormed. "Perhaps it was my fault! All this awful thing!" and she pointed towards the smoke.

"Don't be silly," he said soothingly, now thoroughly alarmed at her pallor. "How could it be your fault?"

"Don't you understand? Belle used to say all sorts of things against Uncle Threlby, and I used to listen to her and let her. Marjory told me I oughtn't to listen. But I did. And perhaps she thought that I believed her, and—well, I think I did, just a little."

"Mother says we never ought to believe a single thing we hear," said Roddy, hardly knowing what he said. "But, anyhow, we aren't sure yet that this person did it."

"I am," said Kitty despairingly. "She knew the place so well. My aunt used to be kind to her, and afterwards—well, Uncle Jonathan was not exactly kind to anyone, and he was rude to her once or twice—don't you remember how she mocked about that threepence? She took a horrible spite against him. Oh, if only——!"

"Well," exclaimed a cheerful voice, "this is a grand sight for a summer morning!"

It was a relief to see Birkett's genial face, pouring with perspiration owing to the speed at which he had come.

They blurted out to him the whole story, but when he saw the exciting document he whistled.

"Belle Catteral? That's likely enough. She's been crazed for many a long day, and if she'd been looked after proper, as she ought to have been looked after, this wouldn't have happened. But what is anybody's business is nobody's business, and that's about it. I ken well enough that she had a spite against the Master. I always laughed at her when she started on that rubbish."

Then they took yet another walk round the place, and were only interrupted by a commotion in the distance, a ringing bell, the rattle of metal, and the sound of horses galloping.

"Fire-engine after all," cried Roddy. They rushed along the terrace in time to see the new Morley District fire-engine dash up the drive in a style that was great.

"Giving themselves a bit of a show-off," chuckled Birkett.

And indeed the brigade, having practised at mock fires for nearly two years, was delighted to snatch at the chance of real active service.

The men sprang off the engine and began unwinding the hose piping at express speed.

"You are too late," said Roddy unkindly, as he stared at them with his legs apart and his hands in his pockets.

"Where there is smoke there is fire," said the police sergeant, who had arrived with them.

"Whisht, my lad," whispered Birkett. "Let 'em shoot a drop or two of water, so as they may say they've done summut for their helmets."

But as soon as the firemen had got going, Roddy pulled the sergeant aside.

"There's something you ought to see," and he pulled out the dirty scrap of paper. "We are dead certain that that was written by a crazy old woman named Belle Catteral," and they told him all about it."

The sergeant listened with attention, but with gathering mortification on his face.

"It looks as if that was all right," he admitted.

"Why, what's wrong?" asked Roddy.

"Why, I made sure this was a Suffragette job —and—well, I've wired particulars to London, and I've sent off a man to see if we can't spot a young lady that has been making speeches all up and down. I heard she was stopping with Lady Doughty at the Castle, and—well, Castle or no Castle, duty is duty."

Kitty and Roddy broke into gay laughter.

"Poor Sergeant!" said Roddy. "And we thought the same. It's sad that a crazy old woman has done us out of a bit of newspaper glory."

"It's a proper nuisance," said the crestfallen sergeant, doing his best to control his disappointment. "Well, I'd best have that bit of paper and see what comes of it."

"Bless my life!" exclaimed Birkett, coming up, "I've clean forgot to give my wife's message. She told me she had a bite of breakfast for Miss Kitty and her friend if they'd care to take pot-luck."

"Would my friend like to take pot-luck?" asked Kitty.

"I'll be jolly hard on the pot if I get a chance at it," said Roddy.

"Then come along," said Birkett, "and leave these fellows to their play. I've smelt that much burning stuff in my life that it's no treat to me to watch men teem water over a crazy old woman's bonfire."

And Don, at the sound of the word "breakfast", led the way.

CHAPTER XXVII

A Telegram from Kitty

THE die was cast, and Mr. Threlby did not regret his decision to make a clean sweep of his Westmorland estates.

Indeed, the thought of getting right away was growing more and more enticing, and, now that the plunge had been made and the whole affair was public, he felt curiously relieved from a heavy load of dull misery.

He became suddenly cheerful and genial, and talked openly in the Club of the Canadian plan, and what amazed him the most was the friendly way in which everyone treated him, as though they were welcoming a long-lost friend into their midst. The world was nicer than he had thought, after all.

But though Mr. Threlby had made up his mind to the sale, it was necessary to face the painful task of going back to Threlby End to pick out a few things he wished to take with him. His wife's portrait was the most important, and as he sat at breakfast he made up his mind to go off to do his duty and take a man with him to whom he could give directions.

The post brought him a letter written in school-girl hand which interrupted his meditation, and which he read twice over.

"MY DEAR UNCLE JONATHAN,

"Thank you very much indeed for the beautiful necklace. I found it in my drawer when I went to Threlby End the other day. It is very good of you to give me such a precious gift belonging to Aunt Molly, and Mrs. Webster says that I must wear it when I am eighteen, because at present it is far too grand.

"I hope that you don't mind selling Threlby End very much, and I am sorry if I have been nasty sometimes.

"Your loving niece,

"KATHERINE."

"Poor child!" he thought. He too was sorry that he had been "nasty" sometimes. However, Katherine's troubles would now be over. On Tuesday he would introduce her to her guardian; and after that he and she would start on their independent lives once more.

He lighted his pipe, and was about to ring to order a car, when a telegram was brought in.

"Jonathan Threlby, Club, High Rigg. Threlby End burnt to the ground. Please come. Katherine."

"No answer," he said to the waiter coolly.

He sat still for several minutes, puffing at his pipe.

Then he said with a slow reverence:

"Thank God, that is all over! Now I never need go there again."

Then he re-read the telegram.

"Please come.   Katherine."

What did that mean? How came Katherine to be there? This was most extraordinary—something into which he must look.

He ordered a car to come round at once, and within half an hour he was swinging up his own drive.

He soon saw that the telegram had told him the simple truth. The place was burnt down to the ground.

There had been nothing the firemen could do, except to turn the smoke to hissing steam, and they were already preparing to pack up when the Master arrived.

He chatted to them for a few minutes, heard all they had to tell, thanked them ceremoniously for their efforts, and then asked if anyone had seen Miss Threlby.

"The young lady is down in the kitchen-garden with one of the doctor's lads," said a fireman.

"But she was not sleeping in the house?"

"Oh no, sir! They rode over on horseback this morning early."

The mystery remained, and Mr. Threlby decided, wisely enough, that the best way to solve it was to find his niece.

"Why, there is Mr. Threlby!" exclaimed Roddy.

Kitty was stooping to examine some enormous

gooseberries, and she started as though she had been shot.

"You'd best go," ordered Roddy. "He won't want me poking in."

"Perhaps," agreed Kitty, overcome with confusion.

But this meeting must be got through somehow; so as soon as she was within speaking distance she cried out:

"Oh, Uncle Jonathan! Isn't it awful?"

He gave her a curious answering smile, then, taking her hand, he looked at her keenly. She was hatless, dishevelled, and decidedly grubby.

"I have known more awful things," he said quietly. "But how came you to be here?"

He loosened her hand, and, taking her familiarly by the arm, he walked her off towards the rose garden.

"We rode over early, to choose some exhibits for the Morley Flower Show. I rode Tim's Hop— he is a grand goer."

"I see." He had already noticed her nondescript riding-costume.

"We never got the exhibits. But we found all this."

"Quite enough for one day," he replied, with a grim smile.

"But, Uncle Jonathan, has anyone told you about the paper we found?"

Kitty felt that there could be no peace until she had unburdened her guilty conscience.

"Yes," he said in a puzzled voice. "The men

have a story that Belle Catteral wrote it. It is most unaccountable. Why should she have done such a thing? I cannot make head or tail of it!"

"But the worst of it is that I can!" groaned Kitty. "I know all about how she hated you."

"Hated me? But why, Katherine?"

"I cannot possibly tell you," said Kitty nervously. "Belle used to talk to me a lot, and I let her say things she oughtn't to have said; and now it feels as if all this were my own fault, and I shall never, never, never be happy again!"

"Can't you give me some idea why this poor woman hated me so?"

"Well, she loved Aunt Molly for one thing," said Kitty, hurrying along. "Aunt Molly was always kind to her, and she gave her money and things, and the last time that Belle saw you, you only gave her threepence—she put that down on the paper, you know, and perhaps it preyed on her mind. She used to say that Threlby End was never the same since Aunt Molly died, and that——"

"Don't trouble to say anything more, my dear girl," he said with a strange kindness in his manner. "I think I understand. Belle has done me the honour of burning down my house in compliment to my wife. Is that it?"

"Only she is cracked—she is quite cracked!" insisted Kitty.

"Perhaps we are all a little cracked now and then," he said quietly. He still kept hold of Kitty's arm, and drew her down to the stone seat on which they had once before sat together in the darkness. Perhaps Don remembered too, for he squatted down against Kitty's gaitered legs.

"I suppose that this will be a tremendous loss to you, Uncle Jonathan," said Kitty, breaking a long silence.

"Not so great as it seems. It is fairly well insured; and perhaps, after all, it is an easier way to lose one's possessions than by a sale. But, Katherine, you have lost all your precious things too!"

"Yes, and I am glad!" she cried tempestuously. "I am glad that everything I really loved has gone. I deserved it, and it makes it just a little bit easier to think that I have lost too. Marjory warned me not to listen to Belle's chattering; but I pitied her, and I thought it was a shame for her to live in that tumble-down house—and so it was! But I might have said nice things about you, Uncle Jonathan, only I didn't. And that is all about it."

"At least the roses are not touched by the catastrophe," he remarked, as, reaching out his hand, he drew one down. He cut it off with his knife, peeled away a couple of thorns, and then handed it to the young girl.

Kitty took it from him with a shy smile, smelt its fragrance, and then stuck it in her coat.

"Now we can be happy," he said quietly.

"I didn't understand," she began again apologetically, but he stopped her by laying a hand on her knee.

"Nor did I; so we will leave it at that.   I liked your note; it was very kind."

"I can't think how you could bear to give a horrid little wretch like me Aunt Molly's jewels!"

"She would have liked you to have them."

"But is it true, what they are saying, that you are going off to Canada, Uncle Jonathan?"

"Yes.   I am tired of the old life, and, like you, I want a change."

"I see."   A horrible feeling of pain gripped Kitty.   She felt all lonely and destitute once more. In spite of her uncle's change of manner he did not care about her really one little bit!

Luckily Roddy thought it was time for him to put in an appearance; and at last it was decided that, as the Flower Show was to open at two o'clock, it was time for them to think of getting away.

"I have sent off Kitty's horse with the man," said Roddy, "but she can ride mine."

"Is there any reason why I should not run her over in my car?" asked Mr. Threlby cheerfully.

"Why, that would be the very thing!" exclaimed Roddy, feeling a load taken off his mind.

CHAPTER XXVIII

The Flower Show

THE Flower Show was an immense success—"the best yet", as was said each year that came round. The tables were crowded with exhibits, and as for the public, you couldn't have squashed even a wasp into that schoolroom with any comfort; and the shillings fairly clattered into the basin, which was guarded by Gregory, who looked very hot in his Sunday clothes, yet gay with a rather droopy geranium presented to him by Nell.

"The Lady of the Order of the Bath Chair," as the boys dubbed the stricken heroine, had been wheeled to the school before the doors "opened". Here she was safely cornered at the end of the room, near the "best bunches of wild flowers"; and, with the exquisite Cerberus to protect her, she joyously received the many friends who came up to commiserate with her and hear all about it.

"Nell is absolutely having the time of her life!" Tim confided to his mother. "Doesn't it suit her down to the ground to play the interesting invalid, with Nurse Samson in glorious attendance!"

"Exactly!" assented his mother, "and she

deserves a little glory, for she has played a tire-some game very pluckily."

As for Kitty, she really didn't know herself under this new sense of being at peace with her uncle. The old contrary feeling against all the world was fading away, and in this new life she had not too much time to think about herself.

It must be confessed, also, that she greatly enjoyed being dressed so nicely for once. She felt quite like other girls, for her clothes gave her a fresh confidence, and she now flitted about with a smile in her eyes, an altogether different girl.

"Why, that will never be Mr. Threlby's niece, eh?" asked Mrs. Masterman of Nell as she looked across at Kitty.

"Yes. Isn't she a dream?" sighed Nell. "And she is an heiress too! Her uncle has given her the most glorious necklace! Haven't I dressed her nicely?"

"You?"

Nell nodded. "Me, practically! Now, isn't that bit of black velvet round her neck ducky?"

"The finishing touch! My grandmother liked nothing better than a bit of black velvet round her throat. But what is this about her being an heiress?"

Mrs. Masterman liked to know all the news, and Nell suddenly remembered that she had no business to be gossiping about Kitty's concerns.

"Oh, well, you know a relation has left her a lot of money!" said Nell vaguely. "She is going up to London on Monday to see him."

"But how can she see him if he's dead?" argued Mrs. Masterman.

"Oh, well, I mean, to see her guardian! She hasn't a ghost of a notion what is going to happen to her. Perhaps she'll go to Paris, or he may want to shut her up in a convent, or—or anything!" said Nell, letting her imagination run riot.

"Bless me!" said Mrs. Masterman. "Why, she had a deal better go and train to be a good farmer! If she has money she could buy a farm, and there would be sense in that!" and then she moved away to be polite to someone else, for Mrs. Masterman was a very important personage, and had to be civil to as many people as possible.

Owing to the fire, Kitty's exhibits had fallen through; but Roddy won first prize for the finest collection of named wild flowers, and Tim got a second for half a dozen Langshan eggs.

Florrie Gregory had beaten him, and when he went up to congratulate her he began by suggesting that the judge had cheated.

"Cheat or not, he knows a good egg when he sees one, and I got t' first prize and you got second!" laughed Florrie.

"I guess you had the judge to supper last night and gave him gooseberry pasty!" he answered.

"I say, Florrie," struck in Roddy, "where is Miss Polly Dennison? Is she here?"

"Why, she's yonder!" said Florrie.

And Polly, who had won a prize for butter which her mother had made, came up keen for congratulations.

"I say, Miss Dennison," said Roddy, "aren't you sorry that you didn't have a hand in firing down Threlby End? It would have been a feather in your cap!"

"And instead of being at the Flower Show you might have been scrubbing out a jail!" laughed Tim.

"She may get there yet!" said Roddy solemnly. "They have sent a cavalry regiment after that beautiful Suffragette! I am going to swear in court that I saw her at Threlby End spying out the land, and that you were her best friend, and must have told her where to go."

"How—how dare you!" gasped Polly.

She really looked so awful that Tim dragged his brother off.

"Why, what's wrong?" demanded Roddy. "She must have a jolly uneasy conscience to get upset at a bit of a rag like that! What a joke if it isn't Belle after all!"

"We shall know when Father turns up." For the doctor had gone off with an inspector to see poor Belle and to make up his mind what he thought about her.

"Perhaps!" began Roddy. "I say, *Cave!*"

For behold, there was the Suffragette herself, standing by Nell's chair, laughing and chatting as though there were no such thing in all the district as a burned-down mansion!

The boys could not keep away. They struggled through the press to introduce themselves.

"Then you didn't do it after all?" demanded Roddy.

" Do what?" asked the girl merrily.

" There was a mansion burned down this morning early, and you needn't pretend that we didn't
see you in the garden poking about on Wednesday."

" Really!" she exclaimed. " Then you were the
burglars whom I saw climbing in at the window—
the most horrible evidence——"

" She's got you!" squealed Nell delightedly.
" And you are the rudest——"

" Were you truly in the garden?" asked Tim.

" Most certainly! I told the police so when they
did me the honour of a visit."

" Oh, do tell us!" cried Roddy.

" Couldn't. It would be too unkind."

" To whom?" asked Tim.

" To the police."

" That's all very well," said Roddy judicially,
" but you have to explain why you were in that
garden."

" Oh, well, of course I had a very special reason!
I admit that."

" Didn't we say——" began Tim.

" I was anxious to see the house and the grounds,
because my mother is wanting to buy a property
in this district."

Nell gave another squeal of triumph.

" But now there is nothing to buy," added
Roddy sorrowfully. " It's an awful pity!"

" Who knows what may happen!" said the
Suffragette. " I should like nothing better than to
try to rebuild the beautiful old place."

"Oh, do!" cried Nell. "What fun! And then you could go ahead at the Suffrage like anything round here."

"Worse and worse!" and Tim shook his head mournfully.

But poor Polly Dennison left the Flower Show in consternation, for Roddy's casual joke had filled her with a fearful terror.

She denied herself all the joys of the dancing and the music, and tramped straight back to Brow Side, to her mother's unbounded astonishment.

As she walked along, she tried anxiously to recall everything she had ever said to the visiting Suffragette.

Polly was not made of heroic stuff, and the more she thought the more terrified she grew. For she now remembered that she had actually said, by way of a feeble joke:

"If you want a good spot to burn down, miss, burn down Threlby End!"

Certainly the young lady had laughed, and retorted:

"My dear young woman, we don't need to burn down houses to get the vote, we shall get it without that."

But, all the same, Polly could not be sure whether there was anything in Roddy's teasing remarks or not, and it was only when the farm servant turned up late that night that Polly knew any peace.

"They've found out who set yon fire going, seemingly," said the man as he lounged at his supper.

Polly trembled so that she had to lean against the dresser.

"And who, then?" asked her mother excitedly.

"Yon daft Belle Catteral! She's cracked, that's what she is! They've took her off to where she will be well looked after, and where they will keep matches and paraffin out of her road."

Polly could have screamed with relief and joy.

She rushed upstairs to her bedroom and gasped out hysterically:

"Then I had nothing to do with it after all! And I'll never, never joke about burning down other folk's houses again!"

CHAPTER XXIX

A Short Sermon

As soon as Mrs. Webster had decided that her visitors had done their duty at the Flower Show, she led them off in an irregular procession along the village street to The Warren.

When Nell arrived, escorted by Tim, Kitty, and Nurse Samson, a great surprise awaited her.

Roddy was standing in the road holding Nimrod's bridle.

"Oh, you darling!" cried Nell.

"Do you mean me or the beast?" demanded Roddy.

"Take your choice," laughed Nell. Roddy had indeed thoughtfully added the finishing touch to her bliss.

Nimrod's knees were still bandaged, but he was really there, and his kind eyes looked at his mistress affectionately as he thrust his nose into her hand.

"See, he has really forgiven me," she cried.

"He is only looking for sugar," teased Tim.

"Then fly for some," she commanded.

So Nimrod was fed and petted, and visitors came

up and wished to hear an exact account of the accident, and again Nell was the centre of interest.

Now Kitty was anxiously on the look-out for the return of the doctor; and by good luck she managed to capture him on his arrival and induce him to come off with her for a private stroll in the orchard, away from the crowd now busily engaged at tea on the lawn.

"Do you mind?" she asked. "You see, I am so aching for you to tell me what happened."

The doctor seemed to understand her anxiety, and, taking her arm in a fatherly manner, he began almost at once.

"It was all very simple. I haven't a doubt that we have discovered a complete explanation of the terrible disaster."

"Yes?" she breathed earnestly.

"I will try to tell you everything," he said seriously, "for you have the right to know. When we arrived at Belle's cottage I left the police officer in the car while I went in alone, and within a few minutes the poor woman confided the whole story to me. Indeed, she boasted gaily over what she had done, and gloated over her own cleverness.

"She seems, so far as I can make out, to have gone to Threlby End late last night, taking with her a can of paraffin and some matches. She found straw in the stable, and, having smashed four windows in different parts of the house, she stuffed the straw inside, poured paraffin over it, and then went round setting light to each lot. She told me all about it, just as a child might talk of a joyful piece of mischief, and she danced about the cottage, clapping her hands, as she described to me how the place blazed.

"It was all quite pitiful, and the story was mixed up with some queer tale of grievance against your uncle—and something about threepence! When I told her that I had called to take her off in a motor to a new home, where everyone would be kind to her, and where she would have plenty to eat and drink, and a beautiful garden full of flowers, she dressed herself up in great pride and came off in perfect contentment. The poor woman is cracked. That is the whole solution of the mystery."

"Poor Belle!" said Kitty pitifully. "Dr. Webster, you don't think it was right, do you, that that poor woman was allowed to live away there alone, without anyone to take care of her?"

"I don't, Kitty," the doctor frankly admitted, "and I had already spoken my mind pretty freely to some of the authorities. You will find out, as you grow up, that neglected duty, no matter what it is, always leads to trouble of some sort, and it does not always seem to fall on the right people either. Neglected ground always has grown weeds and always will. God does not work miracles to prop up our neglect."

"No," Kitty agreed thoughtfully. "You know, I think Belle was truly rather fond of me."

They took the next few paces in silence, and then Kitty remarked:

"It is rather exciting, Dr. Webster, to think that one is really growing up."

The doctor looked kindly at the young girl who had come so unexpectedly into his home, for he was a shrewd reader of character.

"Do you want a little advice, Kitty?"

"I do." She returned his smile.

"Then look straight ahead, and keep your eye on the Guide. Roughnesses will often lie across the path—that is life—but the Guide always leads right. There was once a man who leaped out of a boat to walk to his Master, and he was all right until he began to look at the storm and to calculate his chances. Then he sank! Yet, even when he was sinking through his own foolishness, the Master put out His hand and saved him. But there, my dear child, one oughtn't to preach sermons to young ladies in white frocks at garden parties."

"I have loved it," said Kitty impulsively.

"I say, Kitty," yelled Roddy, "where on earth are you? Mother wants to know whether you would mind playing them all a tune on the fiddle? That Suffragette seems to be a frightfully swell pianist, and she says she'll jig the piano to match you!"

"Why, of course!" said Kitty readily, and she ran off with Roddy to the house.

"You must do your best, Champion," he said anxiously. "I've bragged a lot about you to every man jack of them."

"I'll try not to let you down," said Kitty merrily. And she didn't.

CHAPTER XXX

The Private Letter

It was on the following Monday that Kitty went off with her uncle to London.

It was all exciting, and Uncle Jonathan was as kind as he could be; and after treating her to a sumptuous dinner in the hotel, he took her off to a real theatre, where she followed the adventures of Peter Pan with rapturous excitement.

But on the Tuesday morning at eleven o'clock the real business began.

Uncle and niece walked together into the mysterious region of Lincoln's Inn, went up some dull office stairs, and, after a few anxious moments of waiting, Kitty was introduced to her new guardian, Mr. Marmaduke, and Mr. Threlby, after making some feeble excuse, left them alone together.

Kitty was clearly nervous as she sat in the deep leather-backed chair, facing the lawyer, who was seated sideways to his desk. Yet Mr. Marmaduke was an elderly man with a kind face, of whom no one except a rogue need have been afraid.

"Now, Miss Threlby," he began cheerfully, "the sooner you and I get to understand one another the better. I want to fall in with your ideas, so far as

I can; and for a young lady with money of her own there is a wide choice of plans."

"Yes," said Kitty seriously. It sounded so very strange to think that "a young lady with money" really meant Kitty Threlby, the beggar of the school!

"Perhaps you would first like to know how much there is?" he said, smiling. "Well, I have gone into the figures, and, so far as I can judge at present, there will be funds to bring you in something like a thousand pounds a year!"

"Oh!" If he had said twenty thousand it could not have been more startling.

"But of course," he went on, "I should consider that it would be absurd to spend all that income on a young lady of your age; so, to get to my point, I would suggest that you should be placed in some nice family where you will be happy. I should pay an ample board for you, and supply you with a suitable allowance for your clothes and your private expenses. It is most important," he went on, as Kitty made no comment, "that you should learn the proper use of money—how much it can do and how little. You have not, perhaps, been accustomed to much money?"

"No. Only, when you have been very poor you learn a lot," said Kitty vaguely.

"Most certainly," he said cheerfully. "And now that I have told you my ideas, may I have yours? Is there, for instance, any particular line in life that you would like to take up? Perhaps you have some special talent?"

"I am quite stupid—except about the fiddle. I should like to go on with music," admitted Kitty.

"That will easily be managed, I am quite sure. We might look out for a first-class school. Would you object to a school?"

"I don't mind," she said indifferently.

"Really," thought Mr. Marmaduke, "perhaps the girl is stupid after all. Unless there is something at the back of her mind which she won't let out."

"Your uncle mentioned to me that perhaps you might like to live with Dr. and Mrs. Webster of Morley."

"If my uncle thinks that would be a good plan, of course I do," said Kitty, still without any enthusiasm.

"I didn't gather that your uncle wished to force you to anything. He told me that his only care was that you should do what would really make you happy. Was he wrong in thinking that you had already learnt to like Mrs. Webster?"

"Oh no! I like her immensely." But all the time Kitty was growing redder and redder, until the lawyer began to feel that it was positively unkind to look at her. He began fumbling amongst the papers on his desk.

Clearly he was hurting the girl's feelings in some way. But how? That was the puzzle.

He decided on a change of subject, and, turning to his desk, he brought out a letter and handled it doubtfully.

"Here is a letter, Miss Threlby, about which

I am strangely puzzled. I found it amongst your father's papers, and it was addressed to your mother. As it is marked 'strictly private' I have hesitated to open it, and yet it may possibly contain matters of importance which I ought to know. I wonder whether you would consider that I should read it?"

"I consider!" faltered Kitty.

"Suppose you open it. I expect you would know at a glance whether it ought to be read or be burnt."

He laid the letter on Kitty's knee. She took it and turned it over several times, and at last broke the seal.

It was so strange to think that she was actually to read something written by her dead father.

But after glancing down the first page she stopped short. "I think it ought to be burned," she said anxiously.

She had seen enough to know that it was a pathetic letter to her mother, asking for forgiveness for the wrong done to her. Now that her mother was dead no one in the wide world ought ever to read such a letter.

But a separate slip fell from between the sheets which caught the lawyer's eye.

"This looks like some sort of a business paper," she said as she handed it over.

The lawyer read it through, and his face changed.

"Why, what is it?" asked Kitty, as she replaced the sacred letter in the envelope.

"This is what is called an I O U. It appears that your father owed your uncle a very large sum of money——"

"How much?" interrupted Kitty. Her cheeks paled.

"Well—if true—the sum would cover nearly two-thirds of your fortune."

Kitty sat back. Her father owed Uncle Jonathan money!

Yet Uncle Jonathan had never once hinted at such a thing; and all this year she had thought of him as a mean miser, grudging her every six-pence.

Kitty felt that she would like to have sunk down into the ground with misery.

But her mind was made up at once. Of course every penny of this money must be repaid.

"Uncle Jonathan will know if it is true," she said slowly.

"Yes." Mr. Marmaduke looked at the young girl keenly. "You understand that if it is true, and this money were repaid, it would reduce your income to quite a small sum?"

"It wouldn't matter if it took every penny, if my father owed it," said Kitty proudly.

"Perhaps you are right; but there may be legal difficulties."

"How can there be?" demanded Kitty eagerly. "If we can prove that my father owed it, fifty thousand difficulties cannot stop me from paying it back! I will never touch a farthing of it! I never wanted it, and now—no, never—never!" she added incoherently.

"Well, we poor lawyers must see what we can manage," he said sympathizingly. "But now, leaving this matter for the moment, would you object to my seeing what arrangements I can make with Mrs. Webster?"

"Oh no, write to Mrs. Webster at once, please! It will be a splendid plan for me to go there, if she will have me. I should love it."

Again Mr. Marmaduke was puzzled.

Why should the girl be so suddenly anxious to live at Morley?

Perhaps it was a relief to them both when Mr. Threlby returned and the private chat was over.

Kitty sprang up, and seizing her uncle's arm she said eagerly:

"Uncle Jonathan, did my father owe you a very large sum of money?"

Mr. Threlby stood back, looked from Kitty to Mr. Marmaduke in astonishment, and the blood slowly mounted to his forehead.

"We have found this amongst some papers," explained the lawyer quickly, "and if it is true——"

Mr. Threlby took the paper. It did not take him a moment to read it.

"You must have every penny back!" Kitty burst out impatiently. "I won't touch——"

"Nonsense!" said Mr. Threlby coolly. He tore the paper across and across and across and threw it out through the open window, where the wind caught the fragments and whirled them away.

"Oh, what have you done?" cried Kitty.

"Nothing, my dear child, except that I have made the street rather untidy—disgraceful, wasn't it?"

Kitty stood there speechless, looking after the dancing scraps of paper.

She took no notice as Mr. Marmaduke and her uncle discussed whether it would be a good plan to write to Mrs. Webster, but at last her uncle touched her on the shoulder. She turned, wished good-bye to Mr. Marmaduke, and presently found herself walking through a quiet court in silence, until her uncle suggested that they should rest on a seat in the Temple Gardens.

Kitty sat down nervously enough, for she could not make up her mind what she wanted to say to her uncle.

"Things are clearing up nicely, Katherine!" he said at last cheerfully. "I hear that you are quite willing to live with Mrs. Webster if she will be so kind as to accept such a terrible charge. You will have pleasant companionship, and — well, everything you want."

"Yes."

"I expect we can arrange for you to have a horse of your own too," he went on.

"Yes," said Kitty indifferently.

"You are sure that you will be happy there?"

"Oh yes, Uncle Jonathan, perfectly happy!"

"Katherine, what is it? What is the doubt in your mind? You say you will be happy, yet your voice sounds as if—well, as if I were sending you to prison!"

Kitty gave a horrible little laugh.

"Of course I must be happy—happy as a queen —if you don't want me any more!"

The hot words broke from her passionately, and she dug her poor umbrella so fiercely into the gravel that she smashed it.

But at her words her uncle laid his hand upon her knee and looked into her face with astonishment.

"Katherine, you cannot possibly mean that you would rather go with me to Canada?"

"Not if I would be a bother!"

Mr. Threlby rose excitedly, and, grasping her arm, he absolutely pulled her up from the seat.

"Katherine! Why, my dear child—— Come, let us go back at once to Mr. Marmaduke! Even I cannot take you out of the country without your guardian's leave—they might put me into jail!"

"That would be a frightful shame!" said the girl, scarcely knowing what she was saying.

Could it be true that her uncle wanted her, that he would like her to go with him?

She had to hurry to keep up with him as he retraced his steps to the lawyer's office.

"Katherine," he said, as he paused at the door, "you are sure you mean this?"

"Well," said Kitty, "you see you have only me, and I have only you, and it seems—well, silly for us not to be jolly together!"

"Of course it does!" he said radiantly. "And you could learn to break in horses."

"Fifty thousand!" she laughed.

"And after we have been in here——"

"Yes, Uncle Jonathan?"

"We must go off at once and buy a new umbrella!"

CHAPTER XXXI

Amongst the Old Haunts

"And now, where next?" asked Mr. Threlby as they came out of the umbrella shop.

"Of course, Uncle Jonathan, if you don't mind awfully, I should frightfully like to go and see my two best friends in London."

"And who may they be?"

"Well, there's Mr. Roper at the Riding School. He's good right to the bottom of him. He taught me to ride, and my mother worked for him in the school; and afterwards, when she couldn't any more, he helped us through."

"Then we must certainly see him," said Mr. Threlby. Yet it gave him a pang to think that it was a riding-master and not he who had helped the mother and daughter through. But it was no use thinking of that now, and Mr. Threlby made up his mind that he would now do what he could to make up to Kitty for the pain that was past.

"And then there is Mr. Steiner," said Kitty. "He gave me the fiddle, and I promised that if ever I came back to London I would play to him."

"Then I suppose we must fetch the fiddle," said

Mr. Threlby. " Now I understand why you brought it with you! We will have some luncheon at the hotel and then start out again.   You and I seem to be quite busy people."

"Quick, then, that bus!" cried Kitty like a true Londoner.

" No, we'll take a taxi," said her uncle.

" But that would be a wicked extravagance!" she exclaimed.

"Then let us be wickedly extravagant," he laughed.

The taxi came twisting round to them as if they were the most important people in London, and in they got and were whirled away.

But this was not the only taxi ride Kitty got that day, for after luncheon Mr. Threlby ordered another, and actually kept it waiting all the time they were in the Riding School.

What a joyful excitement it was to Kitty to conduct her uncle down the untidy yard leading to the school, and to open the office door with all the freedom of the old days!

"Mr. Roper!"

The man leaped up from his desk and pulled his cigar from his mouth.

What handshakings and explanations went on, and Mr. Roper looked with undisguised admiration at the young girl in the pretty cream - coloured costume.

"And have you got Bobby, and Firefly, and Tomboy, and Mary Ann, and Queer Fish, and all of them?" asked Kitty eagerly.

"Come and see," laughed Mr. Roper. "She's not forgotten any of them, sir," he added to Mr. Threlby.

"How could I, the dears?" demanded Kitty.

"My word, sir, but you've given the young lady a grand touching-up in Westmorland! She'll have shown you some grand work over them Westmorland fells!"

Now, considering that Mr. Threlby had never once offered his niece a seat on a horse, this was rather an awkward question, and Kitty came generously to her uncle's rescue by breaking in:

"Ah, but what do you think, Mr. Roper! My uncle and I are going right off to Canada to break horses! They will be the wonder of the Empire!"

"Canada! You don't mean that now?"

"Every word! And we shall ride on white horses all the way there too!" chaffed Kitty.

"Well, you'll have to let me know your lowest prices for them when they're fit," said Mr. Roper, with a businesslike nod.

"Rather!" laughed Kitty. And off they went to visit the stables to see the old favourites and the new arrivals. But at last Kitty thought of the taxi, and indeed it was time she did, for after they had wished the riding-master good-bye, they found that the taxi had ticked itself up to nearly ten shillings.

It was awful, yet Mr. Threlby only laughed. But when they reached Mr. Steiner's, Kitty, feeling that she had suddenly become responsible for a mad uncle, made him pay up and send the cab away before they entered the queer old shop.

"Let's pretend that we want to buy his books!" whispered Kitty.

"Please, how much is this?" said Kitty solemnly as the old man came peering out.

Mr. Steiner took hold of a grubby little book on rabbit-keeping, and was just saying "Two pence, miss," when he looked up.

"Why, it's never——"

"Yes, it is!" cried Kitty.

Down went the rabbit book, and the old man and the young girl were wagging each other's hands up and down at a great rate, while Mr. Threlby looked on.

"And this is my uncle," explained Kitty. "Is there room for us both to come in?"

Of course there was room. So in they went, and, in passing, down went a pile of books.

"Never mind them!" said the old man eagerly. "They'll get picked up before anybody wants to buy them."

"And you've fetched her too!" and he seized the old fiddle-case.

"Yes, she's a darling, and she has been as good as gold all the time!" said Kitty.

"And as sweet as ever too?"

"You shall hear! You don't mind very much, do you, Uncle Jonathan, if I play a few little things?"

"No, no!" he said quietly. He sat down on the edge of a chair already piled with magazines, and Kitty tuned the fiddle and then played her very best to her tiny audience.

"She's better! She's better than ever!" cried the old man enthusiastically. "Eh, little lady, you'll make England cheer yet!"

"Not England! I am going to Canada with my uncle," explained Kitty. "And I wanted to know, Mr. Steiner, whether really and truly I may take her with me, or whether you repent?"

She held out the fiddle towards him.

"There is no reason why my niece should not have a new fiddle," began Mr. Threlby.

"A new one!" broke out the old man scornfully. "A gift is a gift. She's welcome to take her round the world, and let her sing all the way if she likes!"

"I'll carry her right off into the sunset!" cried Kitty. "Oh, it is good of you!"

"What is all this noise?" called a grating voice.

It was Miss James, the landlady, who appeared in the doorway carrying a string bag bulging with onions and bananas.

"It's me!" cried Kitty; "and this is my uncle!"

"Well I never!" gasped Miss James, for she was fatter than ever and rather breathless.

So there were more handshakings and explanations, and when at last it was time to separate, it was a puzzle how ever they managed to do it.

"Let's walk," said Kitty, as they at last left the shop. "You see, I know all this part, and every scrap is so interesting. It's like coming back to an old dream."

"Let us walk, then," said her uncle, as he took the fiddle-case from her.

"You see, this part round Islington is sacred to

John Gilpin," explained Kitty. "I wonder how he would manage to get through the traffic now."

"I wonder indeed," and Mr. Threlby smiled.

"It was awfully good of you to bother to listen to the fiddle," said Kitty. "I know you hate music so."

"Why do you think that?" he said quickly, turning upon her.

"Why——" She stopped short, startled at his manner.

"My dear, you are mistaken. Your Aunt Molly loved the fiddle, so how could I hate it?"

Kitty flushed deeply.

"I'm so sorry, Uncle Jonathan," she said softly. "I didn't know."

"I think you and I have not known a good many things we might have known," he said quietly. "And now, Katherine, is there anywhere else you would like to go?"

Kitty looked at him intently.

"Of course, there is one place——" she faltered.

"Where your mother was buried, my dear?" he asked kindly.

Kitty's eyes blinded with tears. She could not speak.

"We will go," he said taking her arm.

Then he called yet another taxi.

CHAPTER XXXII

Auld Lang Syne

THE holiday month of August had come in, bring
ing with it new plans and separations.

Nell and her father were going off to the High-
lands to visit relatives; Dr. and Mrs. Webster
were taking the boys on a wild adventure to the
Isle of Man; and Kitty was to meet her uncle in
Liverpool, to embark on a still wilder adventure to
Saskatchewan. Happily she was to be fully pro-
tected by the redoubtable Don.

But to-day the whole village was quite as excited
as on the day of the Flower Show, and early in the
afternoon men, women, children, and dogs paraded
the road, past The Warren, past the Pump House,
and onwards until they turned in at the Fold Field.

The great Morley Model Village Scheme was to
come off at last, and on this glorious Saturday the
first sod was to be cut by Miss Eleanor M'Leod
herself.

Crowds of interested people from round about
came to wish the Scheme success, and the tem-
porary platform looked as if it would give way any
moment, as the Doctor took the chair, punctually at
three o'clock.

It must be confessed that the speeches were long

and might have been more interesting, but, as Roddy whispered to Kitty from the back of the platform: "One has to put up with this kind of thing in a good cause."

Mr. M'Leod spoke, so did the Vicar, so did a Wesleyan minister, so did the Schoolmaster, so did several leading villagers.

The sun came blazing down on their backs, and the boys wriggled uncomfortably as they felt their clothes sticking to them.

"Another!" groaned Roddy as the sixth speaker rose.

"Hush! They must all have their chances, poor things!" said Kitty warningly; "they are men, you know."

But at last, to everyone's relief, the "platform" descended, and walked in procession to a certain spot which had been agreed upon, and the crowd pressed closer.

Nell, with her arm still bandaged, but looking otherwise fit and bonny, was offered a spade, and amidst breathless attention she managed to stick it into the ground with her left hand and hoist up quite a respectable sod.

"They had loosened it before," Tim remarked, giving the show away.

"And Nell has been practising at it for days," added Roddy.

"I declare with the greatest pleasure that the Morley Model Village is now well and truly begun," cried Nell bravely. This was indeed all that she was expected to say, but the cheering crowd was so

inspiring that she could not help adding enthusiastically:

"And I hope you will all like your new homes
tremendously when you get them, and that the
builders will hurry up, and that everybody will live
in health and happiness for ever and ever."

As Nell stood back there was a wild outburst of
cheering, clapping, whistling, and baby-squealing,
chorused by the aggravatingly excited barking of
the assembled village dogs.

Then the ten-year-old son of the schoolmaster
was pushed forward, looking as if he were deep in
measles, to present Miss Eleanor M'Leod with a
lovely little silver spade, engraved with the date.

At that there was more cheering than ever, and
the band struck up "God Save the King".

But did that cheerful tune mean that everything
was over? Rather not! Morley would have felt
disgraced indeed if it could not have done better
than that.

Instantly the younger people fell to sports, including quoiting, racing, leaping, and wrestling.

Roddy's Champion distinguished herself by win-
ning a prize for the high jump for all comers under
sixteen, to Nell's great delight.

Nell was indeed generous in her applause as she
walked round hanging on her father's arm, watching eagerly.

"Sorry you can't go in for any of these things,
little girl!" said he affectionately.

Nell gave a chuckle.

"It's just as well, Daddy! Kitty is keeping up

the honour of the sex, and I might have let it down with a bang!"

Tim won grand applause in an obstacle race, but ruined a flimsy costume by trying to swarm up a greasy pole to win a leg of ham for the family breakfast.

Perhaps if he had won that ham the reproaches might not have fallen so thickly upon his head.

Yet even the sports did not end the celebrations. A great meat tea was provided in the schoolroom, and after tea there was dancing in the field, and a huge bonfire was lighted on the fell, and the sky blazed with fireworks provided at Kitty's expense.

And was that the end?

Oh dear, no! Mr. M'Leod and Nell invited the party from The Warren to a kind of separation feast.

Everyone declared that he or she was not in the least hungry, but when he or she sat down, then he or she, including Don and Cerberus, found out that he or she had made a terrible mistake.

The noise at that supper table was disgraceful, and it really seemed as though every joke that had ever been born into the family came hopping out to make sure that it had not been forgotten.

So many healths were drunk in ginger-ale and fizzy lemonade that Mrs. Webster grew pale with anxiety.

"Just one last one, Mamma!" cried Tim as he leaped up and put his foot on the table. "Here's to the health and happiness of Roddy's Champion!"

The toast was drunk with enthusiasm, and Tim cried out:

"Up you get, Miss Katherine Threlby!"

"Roddy can," laughed Kitty.

Roddy sprang up, ready for anything.

"Ladies and gentlemen, on behalf of my Champion I thank you all jolly well for drinking this toast. If I may say so, she has grandly kept up her famous reputation this day. Where would the Freckly One have been at that bar, I should like to know? Simply not in it—I mean over it! Bless my Champion's little heart! May all the luck of the world come to her! And remember this, ladies and gentlemen, and especially gentlemen, she is mine, bagged by me for ever! Some day I shall sail across the briny deep and bring her back to Westmorland as my blooming bride!"

Roddy shot down into his seat, mightily pleased with himself, and under cover of the noisy applause, he whispered to Kitty:

"I haven't happened to ask you about the bride business; but that's all right, isn't it?"

"Oh, rather!" laughed Kitty.

"Should Auld Acquaintance be Forgot!" piped up Nell.

They rose with one accord and sang the dear old ditty over and over again, until Don and Cerberus began to bark so exasperatingly that in defence of the family ear-drums it was necessary to stop.